What was beautiful

and

good

What was beautiful

and

good

Jill Blocker

What was Beautiful and Good

Copyright © 2023 Jill Blocker

1st edition

All rights reserved.

Cover design: Jill Blocker

Cover image: Emmy Hennings, courtesy Schweizerische Literaturarchiv

ISBN: 978-1-916964-33-4

Printed in USA

www.jillblocker.com

For Eric(h)

Contents

Prologue, or Patience

Ticino, Switzerland
May 1934

Emmy leaned over her desk to pick at a sliver of wood, piercing the bed of her nail. A single piece of paper lay beside her—a letter from *The Neue Zürcher Zeitung*, the newspaper that first announced their little cabaret.

She wasn't so sure she wanted to reply to the interview request. She wasn't even sure she had an answer to the simple question, "Why did you come to Zurich?" It was merely one of those accidents of life she had blindly surrendered herself to. Nearly 20 years ago now. During the early days of war.

She placed her hands on the keys of the machine then lifted them off, observing the space between her fingers and wrists. Bulges of wisdom, crevices of despair. She tried not to complain about life's mortal pains. She knew the good days and bad rushed by like morphine through the veins.

Outside an open window, an Alpine Swift sang an early summer song. The calls echoed down the fireplace and into the corners of the room. Emmy listened as she remembered a story she was told as a child about what to do if a caged bird dies and its spouse becomes lonely. Placing a mirror in the cage, it was said, would imitate the missing one. Emmy had always found the anecdote charming, how the birds could love so easily and confusingly.

She herself had no mirror of love, yet she knew Hugo's spirit remained with her too. He had told her she would always find him near her. Always in her heart. She looked around the home where they lived. He was still present alongside the painted sparrows on the ceiling and in the shadows of the old Tincinese stone. The sun-kissed plastered cheeks of his death mask hung above the mantle alongside photos of The Madonna. Both silent, yet smiling gently.

She tried to remember the day that she and Hugo had arrived in Zurich. What life was like leading up to their departure from Germany. "We'll be like two tightrope dancers in the dark," he had told her, and she begged him they would always stay that way.

As the clock on the wall chimed on the hour, Emmy thought about how time seemed to pass quicker now that she was older. Though she believed eternal life was more precious, she held onto each passing moment tightly.

She wished Hugo was there now, along with their friends. Hardy, Erich, Lottie, Else, Arp, Huelsenbeck, Janco and Tzara. She remembered how they would unite around a podium or a table at a café, discussing social theories and performing on stage.

Emmy looked out the window in front of her, beyond the yard where the birch trees were dancing. Their full, green branches reflecting on the Luganersee, all the way to Italy. Emmy closed her eyes to the azure sky, then bowed her head to pray.

"Stay true to me," she whispered in a songlike entreaty. "Be thankful beneath my eyes and make your will in me."

When she looked out again, she saw only light. The heavens of early May, suddenly burning bright. She remembered the golden promise that came with each day, so tragically hidden on days when it rained.

"How beautiful that is," she thought. "To have patience with oneself like a little bird that goes round in circles, not caring about anything."

It was precisely that longing for freedom, she realized, that had brought her back to the beginning.

ACT I

GERMANY
Autumn 1913 – Spring 1915

"The world and society in 1913 looked like this: life is completely confined and shackled."

- Hugo Ball

"It seemed to me as if life was finally offering its abundance and beauty from all sides."

- Emmy Hennings

1

The Simplicissimus

The shadow of the red velvet curtain enveloped her. It was more opulent and grand than others she had seen. All the theaters in Berlin, Katowice, Hamburg, and Cologne; the cafés and cabarets of Moscow, Budapest, Vienna, and Bern.

She was grateful for this life; to sing and travel as she wished. Even for the nights that weren't so glamorous. Ones that ended up in sin. The theater scene in Frankfurt, especially, had left her feeling she'd be cleaner on the streets.

It was all just by chance that she was in Munich. She had simply chosen a train at random after being released from prison. She didn't know many people in the city, but that, she considered, was for the better, when trying to give ones' self a fresh start.

She stepped onto the stage and shimmied her dress down her thighs. Tonight, she thought, after 28 years of life, she might finally be on her way to, maybe, actually *making it.*

With the cue of a piano, she closed her eyes, then started singing in a slow, lovely pace. The warm glow of the spotlight felt just like the sunshine of spring.

***

"Bravo, darling!"

Emmy was making her way through the sea of tables when a man grabbed her by the waist. She looked down at his hand, thanked him kindly, then swiftly swept from his embrace.

It gave her a strange, tingling joy to live her life through her art, but often, it seemed, it gave people the wrong impression of her. She worried her talents sometimes stood in the way of what she actually needed. Despite what others believed, it wasn't the external splendor that attracted her to the theater. Besides, she thought, as she continued to weave through the crowd, simply being a beautiful person was not an art.

"Emmy!"

Someone from the back of the room was calling her name. "Emmy, love, come over here!" It was Frank

Wedekind, she realized, with his handsome eyebrows and deep stare.

She had been madly attracted to him once, but lately, she was beginning to find him quite dull. She found his critical view of the bourgeoisie too ironic, considering he grew up in a castle in Switzerland.

"Emmy, love," Wedekind said, as she walked over to his table. He mumbled something to the men around him, then turned and smiled back at her. "How are you?"

"I'm fine, thanks," she said, as she leaned in for a kiss on each cheek.

"That's good," he replied. "Have you heard about my play? It's getting rave reviews in the papers. It's a mystery, but modern. The hero, a female Faust. She sells her soul to the Devil in exchange for worldly pleasures."

Emmy looked at Wedekind critically while he continued to praise himself. She had read the play by Goethe and was sure the original was better.

"Yes," she said. "I'm sure it's great." She didn't bother to mention that to her, God and the Devil were one and the same. She believed in unity in contradictions. Besides, she thought, she knew what kind of worldly pleasures Wedekind indulged in. Most of his criticism against the bourgeoisie had to do with their conservative views around sex.

Emmy stood beside the table as Wedekind continued to talk. Then, she noticed his tall, serious-looking friend kept staring at her. He wasn't so distracting upon the first appearance, but she did find it charming how his gaze moved between the crowd, wallpaper, and her.

"Aren't you going to introduce me to your friend?" Emmy asked, interrupting Wededkind's monologue.

"Oh," Wedekind said, "Yes, this is Hugo Ball…" He waved his cigarette in front of the man. "He's a playwright at the Kammerspiele, where *Franziska* is performing."

Emmy smiled. "Nice to meet you, Mr. Ball," she said.

"Please," he said, "call me Hugo." They locked eyes for a second, then Wedekind continued talking.

"I've met you before, actually," Hugo said, pulling his chair to the side. "In Berlin, a few years ago. I saw you sing."

Emmy looked closely at the man, trying to find a familiar trait. He had a long, thin face, wore an ill-fitting suit and had holes in his shoes. She didn't quite recognize him, but she trusted what he said.

"I've heard your name around," he said, "in reputation and echoes."

"I'm sure only good things," Wedekind remarked with a chuckle.

Emmy glared at Wedekind over her shoulder. Now, she considered, would be the perfect time to ask about the rumors of his syphilis.

"I have some of your poems," Hugo continued, ignoring his friend. "I saved them from the paper when I recognized your name."

"Really?" Emmy asked, slightly surprised. "That's so nice. A true fan."

He smiled.

"It is a shame, though, that you had to cut my poems from the paper," she said. "I sell them myself, actually." She reached into the woven basket hanging from her arm and held up a thin book bound in reed grass and silk.

"You see, Mr. Ball, it's customary for artists to sell their work after a performance. Like my book of poems here or these photos of me and the other performers. Did you like Else or Viola, the other singers?" She held up their pictures for him to look at them.

"Yes," he said, looking at the photos. "No, I mean. Your book of poems. I'd be happy to take a look."

Emmy smiled and handed one to him. He gently opened the cover and flipped through the pages. She had written the titles on the top of each one.

"May 1, 1913"
"Budapest"
"Ether-verse"

Next to the verses, she had painted small flowers with watercolors, to cover up the blots of ink that hid small spelling errors.

She watched as he flipped through the pages, then folded her words between his hands.

"Would you like one?" she asked gently.

"Yes," he said, simply. "I'd like to buy them all."

Buy them all? Emmy considered it. She met lots of people each night at her shows, but none had ever made such an offer. It would make for nice extra money, of course, but she also knew everything came at a cost.

"That's very kind," she said, "but you surely don't mean it. What will you do with so many copies of the same poems?"

"I'll distribute them to friends," he said confidently.

"Oh?" She thought about it. "Might you know someone else who would like them?"

"I know many who would."

Emmy didn't know what to say. "Well," she said finally. "That's very kind of you, Mr. Ball. I'm not sure how I can thank you."

Emmy saw him look again at the photos, which she still held in her hand. The one on top was of her in a long dress, in the red glow of the Cabaret stage. Emmy thought about the cost she made from each. Thirty pfennigs. Enough for a kilo of horse meat or two loaves of bread.

"Why don't you choose my next song?" she suggested, putting the photos back in her basket.

The restaurant was getting louder now, which meant the crowd was getting restless.

"How about, 'Only Love is Life'?"

"Oh," Emmy replied, slightly surprised. "Unfortunately, I can't sing that one."

"But sure, you can, why not?"

"Well, I just sang it one hour before."

"Oh," he replied, in a soft, gentle tone. "That's too bad. I think that's the one song that cannot be sung enough."

"Emmy!" Kathy, the owner of the *Simplicissimus,* called out her name. Emmy waved at her, confirming her attention. The woman stood confidently behind the bar, with her familiar half-angry, half-laughing face.

Emmy started to walk away but then turned back toward Mr. Ball. "Ok," she said, sensing his disappointment. "I'll sing it once more, if the audience agrees…"

Back on the stage, Emmy stood between the curtain and the crowd. The air was filled with clouds of smoke from lips and tips of cigarettes. Emmy made the request to repeat the song, and the audience applauded. And through the haze, toward the back, she saw Mr. Ball smiling.

2

Love Life

Emmy rolled off the bed. It was dark inside, except for where the light came in through the windows. She moved toward the rays so it touched her chest and shoulders. She adjusted her corset, twisting it up around her body to mold her into a more fashionable shape.

"Here," Emmy said, walking over to Rudi. "Do you mind pulling it tight? These things are impossible to put on by ones' self."

Reinhold Rudolf Junghanns, or "Rudi," as she called him, was a painter, etcher, and calligrapher, who had traveled the world studying art. He and Emmy had a sort of "mutual partnership," is what they called it, which Emmy appreciated more than lust alone. She modeled for him and served as his muse, and he had introduced her to an editor, who published her first poem.

Emmy stood with her back facing Rudi. She felt him tie the laces around her back. Then he ran his fingers down her neck and shoulders, leaving light lines of graphite on her skin.

"You're a fantastic model, Emmy," he said. "In the purest sense of the word. Anything but well-behaved, yet extraordinarily stimulating."

Emmy smiled, holding her hands over her chest. "Thank you," she said, then leaned in to kiss him.

"I can't believe I wasted so much time on landscapes," he said, turning back to his canvas. "Your body, the light. It's all the inspiration I need."

Emmy blushed. "I'll see you next week," she said, then kissed him again, twice on each cheek.

***

Emmy loved how Rudi painted her; so fiery and bold. But she wasn't sure mornings with so little sleep were the best time for her to pose. Her dreams were rushed between the cabaret and their weekly meetings at nine. Plus, mornings were the coldest. The chill shook her as soon as she stepped outside.

She noticed how happy she was, though, leaving Rudi's studio. Which was nice, she considered, because just a few months ago, she had felt rather horrible. But today, with the sun directly above, she and the city had good vibes and energy.

The sidewalks were filled with crowds of people: boys hawking newspapers, women shopping and flaneuring. The men stood outside the storefronts smoking and talking. Everything was orderly and peaceful, or at least it seemed so.

"Good morning," a small voice said beside her. Emmy looked down and saw a little girl with bright blue eyes and curly brown hair.

"Oh," Emmy replied. "Hello…" She noticed the girl was holding a basket of roses and was holding out her cherub arm, begging for an offering.

Emmy smiled sadly, then reached into her coat pocket in search of a Pfennig.

"You have beautiful curly hair," Emmy said, placing a few coins in her hand. "It reminds me of my little girl. Her name is Annemarie."

The little girl smiled and gave her a flower, then skipped down the corner to charm someone else.

Emmy tried to avoid thinking too much of Annemarie. Leaving her daughter behind was the only thing that made her feel guilty. Still, after much contemplation, she didn't believe there wasn't any other option but to leave Annemarie with her grandmother. Even if Emmy did want to care for her, it wasn't possible to do so with her lifestyle in the city.

She walked along the sidewalk's edge, then stopped abruptly as a car sped by. The exhaust popped and spewed black dust in the air. The men inside held onto the sides, laughing as they turned a corner, almost tipping over. Emmy watched as the car turned toward Max-Joseph-Platz, toward the city center. The open-topped cars were new and expensive, but Emmy wasn't so impressed by the machines. She had ridden in one once, in Budapest, and had bad memories of the evening. To her, it was just noise without melody.

As she walked toward the city center, toward Amalienstrasse, not far from the Simplicissimus, she saw the crowd outside Café Stefanie. It was typical for a Saturday, but still somewhat odd, that so many people stood looking into the windows to watch the men inside play chess.

Emmy walked up next to the men and peered into the glass, but instead of seeing the players, she was distracted by her own reflection: her hair, cut in a short bob, framed her high cheekbones, and she had dark circles under her eyes. She hoped Rudi hadn't depicted her that way.

She rubbed her eyes with her hands and opened them again. Then she saw her old friend Erich, who was watching her from inside. Emmy smiled and waved at him, then went inside and squeezed next to him in a booth.

"And what are you all up to?" she said, kissing Erich on the cheek. He had a full head of shaggy hair and was one of the smartest people she knew.

"Oh, you know," he said, with a wink. "Just plotting the direction of the world's future."

Emmy looked at him cautiously. "How nice," she said. "Make room for me." She took off her coat and placed the rose in a glass of water in the center of the table.

Emmy had known Erich for a few years, since before she had moved to Munich, back before she had gone to prison, when she had first started performing. He had a long reputation for stirring up trouble, and the newspapers had recently listed him among Germany's "most dangerous anarchist agitators."

Emmy, though, knew a different side of Erich. One whom, as a child, dreamed of growing up and being a poet. She liked that he was passionate and defended the rights of other people. Like her, he always wanted to be where life was most colorful, always in the midst of it.

"What are you doing here?" he asked Emmy, as she reached for his coffee.

"Oh," Emmy said, taking a sip. "I was just passing by."

"Hi, Emmy," the man next to Erich said.

"Hi, Hans," Emmy said, smiling. She offered him her hand. She didn't know much about Erich's friend, Hans Richter, aside from his blue aura.

"You look tired," Erich said, looking at his cup of coffee in her hands.

"Yes, well… I didn't sleep much last night. I was at the cabaret until three in the morning, then I had to be at Rudi's at nine."

"Poor thing," Erich said, almost sarcastically. "Maybe you should try being a little less accommodating to everyone who wants you?"

Emmy glared at him. He was just jealous that she was so popular, she thought. Anyway, she tried not to take his opinions against her too personally. Back when they had dated, briefly, he had always told her how she was naive. It wasn't as if she believed love was a causal game, she just also thought it should be spread widely and freely. To her, if one loved properly, it didn't matter where they were and how they got there. Erich never understood that.

"You just missed Wedekind," Hans said, breaking the silence. "He said he saw your show last night with a director friend of his, who was apparently quite impressed."

"Oh?" Emmy asked, looking forward to his further review. He must be talking about Mr. Ball, she thought. She wondered more about his impressions.

"He's a wonderful dramaturge," Hans continued. "A brilliant, genius director. I don't think it would be out of the ordinary to expect something great from him."

"Brilliant and genius?" Emmy asked, a bit suspiciously but also impressed.

"Don't worry," Erich said. "I'm sure you'll get to know him soon enough. Anyway, to more important topics," he slammed his hand onto the newspaper, which was lying on the table in front of him. "Have you seen all this nationalistic reporting? Something has to be done to stop this cultural change instead of adapting to it!"

Emmy read the newspapers, but not necessarily for the current events. She mostly just liked to read to learn the rhythm of new words. Of course, she knew about the big topics, like the war in the Balkans and other such tragedies, but believed she had enough life experience to form her own opinion on world peace.

Erich read the paper seriously, pulling on the hairs of his mustache that fell over his lip. She could tell that he really wanted to take action. He always had a habit of infusing political theories into his art, folding his beliefs within his plays, poems, and other dramatic forms. She didn't fully understand why he was drawn to such controversy, but she had a feeling it had to do with his childhood. He seemed to embrace being a controversial figure in the name of fighting for equality, even when others labeled him a communist or socialist.

A few years ago, after being charged with conspiracy in court, he founded his own newspaper called *Kain - Journal for Humanity*. He spoke out about abuses of authority and against censorship of speech, sharing his belief that all people, especially the outcasts of society, were just as significant and powerful as anyone.

"People need to understand what Communist Anarchism actually is," he said. "The bourgeois press refuses to publish anything controversial. The people don't know that they're suffering under the status quo. They simply accept their fate instead of following their inner rage."

Emmy chewed on her nail as she listened to Erich talk. He believed the people's liberation could be achieved by the uprising of the oppressed and tortured, but Emmy wasn't sure he could make any change on his own. Germany had been censoring speech since the early 19th Century – not just in newspapers, but also in cinemas, cabarets, and theaters.

"I don't know," Emmy said. She finished the last of Erich's coffee. "It seems to me that what people want is easily digestible material. There is enough struggle during the day. People just want to be entertained for a few hours in the evening."

Erich didn't say anything. He just continued staring at the paper.

"I should get going," Emmy said after a few more moments of silence. She stood up with her coat in her arms. "Are you coming to the show on Friday?"

"I'll be there," Hans said, handing Emmy the rose she had placed on the table.

"I'll try," Erich said. Emmy leaned in so he could kiss her cheek.

"Oh, and Emmy..." he said, before she turned away. "Try to get some rest. Your love life is making you look rough."

3

Backstage

Backstage at the Simplicissimus, Emmy prepared for the show. Viola, Else and Lottie all stood next to her alongside a wall of mirrors. She would sing, Viola would dance and Else would recite a few poems. Lottie worked behind the scenes, sewing the costumes for their performance.

Emmy looked into the mirror and lined her eyes with Kohl. She pinched her cheeks to make them blush and accentuate the freckles on her nose.

Viola was brushing her long, blonde hair, which made Emmy miss having long, blonde hair of her own. She ran her fingers through her strands, tugging at the ends.

Lottie sat down on a red velvet sofa with her skirt in her hands. Her stockings were up to her knees as she sewed a rip in her hem. Else, the eldest of them all sat down on a tall bar stool and started spinning back and forth.

"Do any of you know Hugo Ball?" Emmy asked rather suddenly. She wasn't thinking of him specifically. She was just thinking about who might be in the audience.

"The playwright?" Else asked, looking into the mirror at Emmy.

"Yes," Emmy confirmed. "I believe so. He was at the show last weekend with Wedekind. Then, the other day, at the café, Hans Richter was praising him for being a 'brilliant and genius director.'"

"Brilliant *and* genius?" Lottie asked with an overexaggerated breath. She was two years younger than Emmy, but their birthdays were the same.

Emmy laughed. "That was my reaction exactly. But Hans Richter said that it wouldn't be out of the ordinary to expect something great from him."

"Is he handsome?" Lottie asked.

Emmy thought about it. "Maybe not in popular opinion… but I learned after my first husband that looks aren't everything."

"Well," Else said, "It doesn't matter anyway because he's engaged."

"Engaged?" Emmy asked. He hadn't mentioned it.

"Yes," she replied casually. "To an actress in Vienna."

Emmy didn't know what to say.

"Who?" Lottie asked, but Emmy tried not to listen. She didn't care who the woman was. She only cared that Hugo didn't mention it himself. If he was going to buy all her poems and pretend to be interested in her work, he might consider his fiancé's opinion first. Slight pangs of disappointment flowed through Emmy's thoughts.

Lottie stood up and tied a silk ribbon around Emmy's waist.

"Never expect anything from anyone," Else said, as if she were addressing all women, not just them in the room. "Fall in love all you want, but don't become dependent."

Emmy took Else's advice but also knew she just lacked enthusiasm after giving too much of herself over the years. Recently, she was left penniless after a nasty divorce in which her husband left her for a young Swedish painter.

"Oh, don't worry," Emmy said, agreeing with her friend. "I will never again be the private property of a man. I've made that mistake too."

Emmy looked back into the mirror, focusing on herself. She had too much makeup on, which looked good under spotlights but not in the sun. It was true what Erich had said, she thought, looking into her own eyes. Maybe her love life was wearing on her. Smoking ether probably didn't help either. Maybe, Emmy considered, Heroin would be better. She had heard doctors were prescribing it to soothe women's cramps.

"What poem are you going to read tonight, Else?" Viola asked. She finally stopped brushing her hair and sat next to Lottie on the couch.

"Oh, I hope one about love," Lottie said with excitement.

"Yes," Else said, taking a deep breath. "One for a man who has been inspiring me lately."

Emmy looked over at Else, who had on a long dress with a lace collar. She smiled at her friend's hypocrisy but allowed her her opinion. She was ten years older, which meant she should be wiser, but maybe, Emmy thought, when it comes to understanding love, age doesn't matter.

Emmy went over to the curtain and peeked behind the red velvet fabric. A rush of noise and smoky air came inside their makeshift tent. She looked out at the crowd but then locked eyes with Kathi, who was coming toward her and didn't look happy.

"I hope I'm impressed by you girls tonight," Kathi said, holding empty beer kegs in each hand. If anything, she was a strong woman, Emmy considered.

"You will be," Emmy replied, smiling at her. She wasn't sure what Kathi had against her, but she once told her she had eyes like Till Eulenspiegel - a mischievous boy from old German fairytales.

Kathi nodded, then put the kegs outside the back door, then rolled a full one toward the front of the bar.

They all stayed quiet until the owner was out of sight; then, Lottie chose a dress from the rack and helped Viola put it on.

Emmy always loved dressing up and playing different roles. When she was a child, she would perform plays for the neighborhood. One day Sleeping Beauty; another, Snow White, then Venus in the Green, or Ophelia. She loved the stories of heroes and battles and love at first sight and the idea of escaping into a "happily ever after." She wasn't too proud to admit that she still believed that one kiss from a man could open a whole new world.

She wondered again who might be in the crowd, if Erich, or Rudi, or Hugo Ball would be there. She couldn't decide if there was anything wonderfully romantic about any of them, but she knew that she loved love; the being in love, the making of love, all of it.

4

Showtime

Emmy never remembered the smell of a show. She always only remembered the lights and the glow. The shine off the windows and frames on the wall, bouncing in all directions, filling her soul as she sang. She didn't think about much, mostly just about what she was singing. And because she was singing a love song, she thought about love.

She reached the highest pitch, matching her voice to the violins, then held her breath at the top and quickly released it. At the end of the song, she breathed in the mood, then smiled and bowed to the applause of the room.

There was a full house that night, more than 100 people, sitting in wooden chairs around French-style bistro tables. She bowed a second time until the claps settled, then walked off stage to make her customary rounds.

Emmy walked around the tables, looking for people she knew, holding her basket of photos and poems. She saw Wedekind first, at his usual spot, next to Erich, who was sitting next to Hugo Ball, who was staring straight at her.

Unbelievable, she thought. Sure, he was an admired director, but he was also engaged. She turned to walk the other way.

"Emmy!" Hugo called out just as she made her move. She looked back around and saw Hugo set his drink down and got up from the table.

"Emmy," he said, walking over next to her in a hurry. "I've been wanting to talk to you."

Emmy looked at him. There was something cynical in his nature that somehow distracted her.

"Can I buy you a drink?" he asked.

"I'm sorry, Mr. Ball," she said, "but I have other guests…"

"Please," he said. "I need to talk to you about something important."

Emmy was used to such offers and knew better than to fall quickly for the temptations of men. Besides, she found it demeaning to profit from the fleeting desires of others. But somehow, the longer she looked at Hugo, the more beautiful and clever he became.

"Ok," she said cautiously. "One drink."

Hugo stood tall in front of her, at least 6 feet high. His dark hair was cut in a rough fringe too high above his eyes.

"So, today is Saturday?" he asked, handing her a drink. It was a strawberry *Sekt*, which reminded her of summer.

"What do you mean?"

"Your last song," he said. "The words said, 'It's a Saturday evening, and you're waiting at the door.'"

"Oh," she said. She didn't realize one might take the words literally.

"… so tomorrow is Sunday?" He continued.

She thought for a minute. "I suppose."

"Are you sure of that?"

"… No?" Now she was confused.

"Maybe it will be Saturday evening," he said, shrugging. "The world is full of errors, you know."

Emmy tried to understand his point. "Are you a philosopher, Mr. Ball?"

"No," he replied. "I'm a dramaturg."

"Oh yes," she said, "Theater."

Hugo smiled. "It provides me a freedom I cannot find in life."

Emmy nodded in agreement. To that, at least, she could relate.

"Actually," Hugo said. "That's why I came to talk to you. I'm planning my next play, *The Life of Man*, and I want you to star in it."

Emmy wasn't sure she had understood.

"You want me to play?"

"I already know there is no one else suitable for the role," he said.

Emmy thought about the idea. She admired his proposition, though she wasn't fully sure she could trust him. She was honored that he had thought of her, but she was a singer, not an actor. And what if she wasn't good enough?

"Don't worry," he said, sensing her nerves. "I'll be directing it, and it will just be the two of us."

"Yes, but…" she replied. What could she say? She couldn't just pass up such an offer. "I mean… yes. If you're in charge, I suppose that would be okay."

Hugo smiled at her with an innocent self-confident look, then held up his drink in celebration. Emmy took a sip and thought about her decision.

"I heard from Hans Richter that you are a good director," she said.

"And you found it hard to believe?" Hugo asked.

"Oh, no, I can very well imagine that it's true."

She didn't know what to say. He made her nervous in a way that no one else did.

"If you will excuse me, please, Mr. Ball," she said. She took the final sip of her drink and set it aside. "I must be going."

"Can you come back later?" he asked, reaching for her hand.

"I can't, unfortunately," she said. "You must understand. I have other guests to entertain."

"The English Garden then," he said. "Tomorrow at noon? Meet me on the bench by the roses."

"You really believe I can help you with *The Life of Man*?" Emmy asked.

"Yes," he replied. "You can, and you would."

5

The Garden

The next afternoon Emmy met Hugo Ball by the roses. As they sat and read the verse aloud their voices became lost among the thorns and petals. *The Life of Man* was a play about a man and a woman. Two people who were so madly in love they barely noticed they were poor. It was written in a gothic fashion, with dark and frightening elements in the style of Edgar Allan Poe, with just a hint of Romanticism to encourage the reader to fall in love.

"At this point," Hugo said, taking his role as the director, "a light would shine onto the stage. The glow will subtly evoke the actor's inner beauty. Then, where it is bright, the lights turn off, and in that moment, they begin to love."

Emmy tried to envision it.

"Of course," he continued, there's room for interpretation."

Emmy had been flattered when Hugo had first asked her to star in his play, but as she read the story, she found herself uncertain. The storyline was full of secrets, love affairs, and sin. It addressed nearly every secret pleasure that Emmy had taken part in.

She looked at Hugo as he went back to the play. His lips moved quickly across each syllable, leaving little time to breathe.

How could love be private property, she wondered as she listened to the story. Such egoism she could never understand. In her opinion, what belongs to a beautiful world should belong to everyone. Otherwise, the less fortunate would always be left lonely and empty-handed.

As for Hugo, she thought, gazing critically at him. There was something mysterious to his being, which somehow drew her closer to him. Or maybe, she considered, he was just more interesting than the simple-minded woman in the story.

"I'm not a good actor," Hugo said, looking out across the park. "But I definitely need to play." His brows furrowed on his face as he folded the book in his hands. "Emmy?" he asked, somewhat seriously. "What do you think about a hero who achieves nothing in life except to be called 'human'?"

Emmy didn't know how to reply. For her, it was good enough to be recognized as a human, even occasionally. As a woman, she was familiar with the feeling of not being heard.

"Only man can forget that he is a child of light," she replied, brushing aside his concerns. "About this play, though, the more I read, the more I'm worried I'm not right for the role."

"Of course you are," Hugo said. "Why would you think such a thing? It will be easy. As simple as talking to people."

"That's it exactly," she replied. "It might not be easy for me to play simple."

"What do you mean?"

"Well," Emmy said. She leaned toward Hugo and whispered in his ear. She told him what she really thought about the woman in the play and how some desires weren't a sin but perfectly acceptable. At first, he seemed to not understand, but his childlike innocence only charmed her more. She wanted him to pick her, like an apple from a tree.

Emmy moved her lips from his ears to his neck, then wrapped her hands around his arm, moving slowly to his mouth like a bee searching for nectar. As they rolled onto the grass, the birds began to sing, and under the cloudless sky, they escaped the pliable blanket of earth.

6

War

Then there was the war.

Emmy had learned of it when a peasant girl yelled it through the Judas hole. Her voice, with the light seeping through the peephole of the prison's iron door. "*It is war!*"

***

For the past year and a half, Emmy had known things were getting bad. But for a while, she hadn't been thinking of much besides herself. She spent the spring and summer chasing everything that brought her joy. She traveled and sang and did what she could to survive.

Just before her arrest, however, things had taken a serious turn. And quickly, it seemed everything was going wrong, not just for her but for the whole world.

It all started back in June with the assassination of Archduke Franz Ferdinand – the heir apparent to the Austro-Hungarian Empire. He and his wife, Sophie, were visiting Sarajevo on their wedding anniversary. According to the news, the city near the border of Bosnia and Serbia was ripe for conflict, and even the Archduke suspected some protests when they arrived in the city. What he didn't know, though, was that on their way to their event, assassins were lined up along their travel route, which had been published the day before in the newspaper. At least three young men, committed to freeing Bosnia from Austrian rule, were ready to risk their lives to kill the Archduke to fulfill their desire for independence from his rule.

The first man threw a bomb, which rolled off the folded hood of the luxury convertible that the Archduke and his wife were riding in. Their driver sped away, but the bomb landed under the vehicle behind them, injuring 20 more people in the explosion. Safe but shaken, the couple arrived at their event at the Town Hall and afterward wanted to visit the hospital where their colleagues were being treated. A turn down a road to avoid the city center, however, led them face-to-face with another assassin, who shot the Archduke in the neck and his wife in her stomach.

The news headlines vowed that Austria would avenge the murder of the Archduke, which they said was executed by a 19-year-old South-Slavic nationalist. A war with the inhabitants of Serbia and Bosnia was predicted, along with Russia, which was called the "protector of all the Serbs."

The news was tragic, Emmy thought, but she wouldn't have been so affected by their deaths if what escalated in the following weeks hadn't affected nearly everyone she knew. Germany, who was allied with their Austrian neighbors to the south, immediately started calling men to the front. Even *The Life of Man* had been called off when Hugo volunteered to fight.

For the whole month of July, Europe was in crisis. Then, countries all around Europe started to declare war on one another. First, Austria-Hungary against Serbia for the death of the Archduke. Then Germany declared war on Russia, standing behind Austria. Russia, which had a long-standing presence in the Baltics to gain access to trade routes in the Bosphorus Strait, was seen as the biggest threat to Germany, which saw itself as the leader of the Central Powers.

Russia was an ally of France, and the Germans immediately feared a French invasion. So, in a plan to catch Paris off-guard, they crossed through neutral Belgium. The Belgians didn't want German troops to cross through their land, but because – like the Swiss – they abided by the "Law of Neutrality," they didn't have a military to prevent it. The "Schlieffen-Plan," as the news had called it, may have worked if the British, under alliance to protect Belgium, didn't declare war against the Germans.

Soon, Germany declared war on France, England declared war on Germany, Germany declared war on Belgium, and Austria-Hungary declared war against Russia.

Emmy could barely keep up.

***

She rolled over on the bed, which was just a thin mattress on the floor. Moonlight shone through the bars on the windows, leaving shadows on the gray wall. She tried to imagine her life as a novel, with a narrator guiding her path, but instead of finding any hope, all she could think about was dying. It was as if an angel of death stood in her room, offering her a final escape from her sorrows.

Maybe she was better off dead, she thought, even though she didn't know exactly why she had been arrested. She closed her eyes and tried to think of what she could have done. There were an infinite number of sins she could attest to, but none that she believed she was caught doing.

She had been at the Simplicisimus when the officers arrived. She had gotten into a fight with Kathi earlier that day about singing a patriotic song. She couldn't sing in German; she told Kathi. Not because she wasn't German herself, she had told her, but because she believed the language lacked infatuation and tenderness.

Re-thinking all the tragic events made her heart weaken.

She rolled over again and turned her face toward the wall. Maybe she should pray, she considered, even though she wasn't sure she deserved God's divine grace and forgiveness. Still, she thought she could ask him for a favor. She wished not to escape the world but dance until she was short of breath.

7

Patriotic

"Are you going to tell me my charges?" asked Emmy.

The warden pulled clothes from a drawer and threw them in Emmy's arms. A bright-pink tulle skirt overflowed onto the floor.

"You'll be informed of your trial date in a few weeks," the warden said. "You can change in the toilet." She pointed to a door at the back of the room.

"Trial for what?" Emmy asked. "You can't just hold me here for weeks without telling me why."

"Of course, we can," the woman said with a smirk. She was tall and weathered and had a tough exterior. Looking at her, Emmy was convinced that if she had enough time, she could make her fall in love with her.

But the clock on the wall read 11:23, and she preferred not to spend one more minute in jail.

After changing her clothes, Emmy gave the gray uniform back to the warden and stepped outside the prison in high heels and a pink skirt. It was comforting, she thought, to be in her own clothes again. She ran her fingers through her knotted hair and turned her face toward the sun. Its radiance, one of the few things in life that she could always rely on.

Emmy walked along the street, her skirt blowing in the wind, feeling more like a princess than a woman who had just been in jail. The September air was light and friendly, which made her quite happy, but then again, she still wasn't sure what she should do next. She couldn't just go back to her apartment, she thought. She had already spent weeks by herself in a room. So, she stopped inside a café to sit for a while.

The restaurant was busy with diners ordering lunch, so the waiters didn't notice when she sat down at a table in the corner. She moved aside an empty mug and saucer, then leafed through a newspaper that had been discarded on the table.

War, according to the headlines, had become a "Race to the Sea." The Germans were winning over Russia, but the Russians were faring well against Austria-Hungary. Germany's Chief of Staff was quoted in an article that he believed in a "hard, offensive war." And even though it was autumn, and the cold and rain were coming, the troops were ordered to continue through Belgium and fight their way to the Northern Sea.

Germany had lost the Battle of the Marne, which meant Paris had been saved. The news reports called it "one of the most important battles in history." The French, according to the papers, had hired more than 600 taxis to transport their army through the city.

Emmy looked at the photo, running her fingers over the print. She had seen the taxis the last time she was in Paris. The Renault carriages were black and white in the picture, but she could remember how bright yellow the rims were. Young soldiers were piled in the open-top cars and the two men at the back were smiling at the camera.

The taxis gave the French an edge, according to the report. But even though they won the battle, the Germans held the upper hand, it said. Now the front extended 400 miles, all the way from Switzerland to the coast of the North Sea.

***

"Hard to believe, isn't it?"

Emmy looked up, half-expecting to see the waiter, but instead saw her friend Hardy beside her.

"Hardy?" She could hardly believe it. Tears swelled in her eyes.

"Emmy," he said. Emmy stood up to hug him. "How are you?" He kissed her on each cheek.

Emmy hadn't seen Hardy in years – since their vacation together in Paris when she fell ill with Typhoid. They had met a few years prior, and Emmy had fallen in love with him. He had a way with words, as well as his fingers.

Emmy smiled at him, suddenly embarrassed by her appearance. She was wearing an evening gown in the middle of the day, and she was sure her hair needed some attention.

"Do I look as bad as I did when I was sick?" she asked, combing her fingers through her bangs.

"I only have good memories of Paris," Hardy said. He sat down across from her and raised his hand for a waiter. He took off his scarf and newsboy cap and placed them on the table. He had a serious look but with a diabolic elegance. Emmy wondered for a second if she might still be in love with him.

In Paris, they, like the city, were full of dreams. They had gone up the Eiffel Tower, taken an evening boat ride on the Seine, and watched the painters at Montmartre and a show at the Moulin Rouge. Emmy found the French performers more exotic than the Germans, and she had taken notes on their refinement and elegance.

"Do you think it's still the same?" Emmy asked with tears in her eyes. So much had changed in just a few years.

"Nothing ever stays the same," Hardy said. He turned away from her to place his order with the waiter.

When Hardy had left her in Paris, she was still ill at the hospital. He said he had to go back to Berlin, where he worked as a stenographer transcribing reports from Germany's government. Emmy was left alone, losing handfuls of hair and becoming thin. She thought she might die, but then she prayed to God and promised to become a devout Catholic if she survived.

"So, how are you?" Hardy asked, taking a sip of his coffee. He looked at her up and down. "Did you just come from the theater?"

"Prison, actually."

"Prison?" he asked, finally taking an interest.

Emmy told him all about the past few weeks and the few years before. Where life had taken her since the last time she saw him. She told him about the arrest and how she didn't know what she'd done wrong, how she had just been doing her job when she was put in prison. Hardy listened, knowing some of what she'd gone through. He was the one who had helped her get her first job at a cabaret when he translated a French song for her to audition with.

"And now I'm here," she said. "What about you?"

"Well…" he said cautiously. "I'm glad you're okay. I've been fine. I just got engaged."

"Engaged?" Emmy was surprised. She had only always considered Hardy's love for her.

"Oh," she said. "Congratulations." She tried to make it sound as if she were happy for him, but now all she could do is think about what life was like when she was in love with him. When they were dating, he had told her she would always be his muse, and she had dedicated her first poem, *Aetherstrophen*, to him. She had written it while they were high on cigarettes dipped in Ether. Hardy said it inspired him intellectually, but it just made her feel like she was flying.

She missed the carefree nature of their love and how they drew inspiration from each other.

She looked at him, trying not to cry. Then, he told her that he must get going and called the waiter for the bill.

He kissed her on each cheek before walking away and left her without arranging a date to meet each other next.

***

For the next few days, Emmy stayed in bed. At least there, she thought, nothing bad could happen to her. Life had been too unpredictable since the war had begun.

She lay there in a dazed state between sleep and awake, only getting up to eat and wash her face.

She thought about Hardy every day, about how he hadn't chosen her and wondered if she was unlovable.

Maybe she hadn't been intelligent enough, or he didn't find her pretty. She turned on the faucet, splashed water on her face, and looked at herself in the mirror as water dripped down her cheeks. No, she thought, that wasn't it. He had always been jealous when other men paid attention to her.

Maybe she should go back to the cabaret, she thought. She always felt better when she was on stage. The instant sense of dignity, acknowledgement, and pleasure.

As she washed her hair, she took some time to remember the things she was grateful for; her curiosity and creativity and passion for love and freedom. Deep down, she knew what her strengths were and what she must do to get up and take on the world.

Emmy wrapped a towel around her body and another around her hair. She would go back to the Simplicissimus, she decided, and ask for her job back.

***

"Please, Kathi, you can trust me."

Kathi wasn't even looking at her. She was just rushing back and forth behind the bar, filling drinks and taking orders.

"Just one song at the end. I promise the audience will love it."

"No," Kathi said, stopping to look Emmy in the eyes. She put down the four steins of beer, which she had intertwined between her fingers.

"Why not?" Emmy asked. "Are you still upset that I refused to sing that old German song? I can sing in German, Kathi if we must choose politics over friendship."

"No," Kathi said. "It's not possible, I'm sorry. There's no place for you here anymore." She turned her back to Emmy and reached for a bottle of rum.

Emmy looked at the stage where two young women were dancing. She didn't recognize their faces or the sound from the piano. The audience was different, less energetic, and older. More men in suits and top hats smoking cigars, looking tough and important.

Without saying goodbye, Emmy turned away from the bar, leaving the Simplicissimus feeling more defeated than before. The café was once a place for bohemians and foreigners, but now modern art and literature were becoming more conservative. It was as if everyone was trying to outmaneuver the other – both in love and war. They feared what might come the next night or day.

Emmy walked out of the café and looked up into the sky. It was too quiet, she thought. She had read in the paper that morning that citizens should be afraid of bullets falling from the sky. A recent British air raid had destroyed a Zeppelin base in Germany, destroying the balloon airships that could hold five machine guns or two tons of bombs.

Emmy couldn't understand such hate and destruction. She wondered if all these men who were fighting knew anything about the other. Have they ever tasted their enemy's cuisine or heard the romance in their language? She longed now, more than ever, to visit all the cities in the paper. Paris, St. Petersburg, Vienna. Cities in the midst of war.

She remembered the stories her father had told her as a child of the places he had traveled. He had gone around the world twice, sailing the ocean like Sinbad the Navigator or Robinson Crusoe. It was his adventurous spirit that stayed with Emmy as she grew up.

She longed for an adventure. Munich, dark and empty, did not seem to reciprocate her energy. Only the lion statues on the Siegestor seemed up for the challenge. Poised, ready to pounce, from the top of the three-arched gate in the middle of the street. How sad, Emmy thought, that a monument of victory meant memorializing tragedies. How many victories did one need before settling on peace?

When she reached her apartment, she wasn't sure what to do next, so she checked her mailbox and tried to keep her faith.

Then – as if a sign from above – there was a letter waiting for her, addressed from Hugo Ball.

8

Back in the Garden

"Emmy!" Hugo shouted as he rushed toward her.

Emmy stood up from the bench where she had been waiting and fell into his chest. His arms wrapped around her.

In his letter, Hugo had asked Emmy to meet him in the garden, at the same spot they had met last summer to read *The Life of Man*.

Emmy hadn't heard from Hugo for so long, and now, as they sat next to each other, he told her where he'd been. He had volunteered for the war with one of his best friends, but despite making it through the training, he was deemed unfit.

"I'm sorry," Emmy said, sensing he was upset. "That's great for you, though, isn't it? That you don't have to fight? Now all you need is the big 'U' on your papers, and you would be permanently unfit and rid of it forever."

"Yes," he said with uncertainty in his voice. "I'm happy to be away from the front, at least for the time being. I'm coming to realize the war is a blatant mistake. Humans are being treated like machines instead of people."

Emmy nodded.

"How about you, though?" he asked. "How have you been?"

"Well," she said, trying to figure out where to begin. "I was in prison, and Kathi won't let me sing." Suddenly, she began to cry.

"I'm fine," she said, trying to catch her breath. But actually, she felt terrible, like her heart had burst open and there was no way to fix it.

"Don't cry," Hugo said, trying to console her. He placed his hand on the upper part of her back.

"I'm innocent, I swear," she tried to explain. "Still, they held me in custody for three weeks, where the fear of death consumed me. I tried to convince myself that I was guilty. I've committed my fair share of sins, of course, but without knowing the charges against me, I can't call myself a criminal."

"Is there something I can do to help?" Hugo offered.

"No," Emmy replied sadly. "No one in the whole world can help me." She was crying loudly now, causing people passing by to stare.

"No one?" Hugo asked. "Are you sure?"

"No," she said. But then she considered it. Maybe if she had someone to love, she would feel better. But she had no one. Even Hardy was marrying another woman. "No," she said. "I have no one. And the one I love does not want me."

Hugo's eyes got wider. "You must be mistaken, perhaps?"

"About what?" Emmy replied. "That someone doesn't love me? Mr. Ball, in such matters, one cannot be mistaken."

"Well," he said. "I don't know…"

Emmy sighed, wiping away her tears.

"But…" Hugo continued. "He who tells you he does not want you… he wants you. Believe me."

No, she thought. Hugo didn't understand. It was about the intensity of love. The strength of the feeling, not the duration.

"Is it really so bad?" he asked.

"Yes," she replied. "It's so bad, even worse. Like a constant toothache, night and day."

"Well, who doesn't love you?" Hugo asked. "Maybe I can convince him. I'll bring him to his senses. Maybe he just doesn't know how much you like him."

"Of course he knows," Emmy said, shaking her head.

"Then, I'll remind him of his duty," he said. "If he doesn't like you, I'll just force him to."

"What good would that do? Love cannot be enforced."

"Sure it can. Under certain circumstances," he said.

Emmy considered it. "Do you really have time to take care of my affairs?"

"Of course, it makes things difficult for me, and I would prefer not to," Hugo replied. "But, I will. I'd only regret it for your sake if I don't."

"Really?" Emmy was surprised. That was the peak of a true friendship, she considered.

"And, when I do bring this man back," Hugo continued, "I'll retire from your side."

"What?" Emmy asked. "But why? We have to stay friends."

Hugo seemed hesitant. His eyes looked out over the park, and his hands were in his coat pockets.

"Please," Emmy said. "At least for a few years. Two or three. Then, we can see."

"Ok," Hugo said, laughing. He looked softly into her teary eyes. "I suppose I can agree to that."

As Hugo shuffled side to side, the sound of broken leaves rose from beneath his feet. The lush green grass they had once rolled around in was now brown and muddy.

"Then, I'll leave you here, Ms. Hennings," Hugo said, standing up and slightly bowing toward her feet. "I'll be in Munich for a couple more weeks, and then I'll be heading back to Berlin. I'm taking a leave from the theater to work as an editor for a newspaper."

Emmy looked up at him.

"I still want to see the war," he said. "Even if I can't fight. I want to go to Belgium and see the front for myself."

"Until then…" He leaned down and put his hand on her shoulder and kissed her forehead. "Take care of yourself… and write if you need me."

9

Café Luitpold

As the days before, Emmy spent the next few days in bed trying to dream up a new future. Her heart still ached for Hardy, but the longer she considered it, she didn't really want Hugo to talk to him. Especially because now, each morning when she woke up, it was Hugo whom she thought of first.

She didn't know why she was suddenly thinking of him. Maybe she just wasn't used to having such noble friendships. He genuinely seemed to want to help her, which was more than Hardy had offered when he last left her.

She should have expected that Hugo's generous offer, his beautiful senselessness, would make her happy, but then, such selflessness was not always desirable. Though, what if Hugo would be successful and could convince Hardy to be with her? No, she thought, her mind spinning with reason. It wasn't right to hurt another person because of one's grief. One should either love a person fully or not at all.

Emmy recalled all the times she had considered giving her heart away. Her mother had always urged her to stay home and get married from a young age. The first time she was asked to marry, it was from a man who taught her the piano, who also happened to be blind. Then, there was the man twice her age who already had six kids. At the time, she had not denied love from either of them, but she did pray to God to give them luck and leave her single.

She was almost 30 years old now. Old, especially compared to the boys half her age who were fighting in the war. Children as young as 15 were marching shoulder-to-shoulder, singing the same patriotic songs that Emmy had refused.

Emmy knew there was no time to waste in life or love. Her heart had been broken before, and she had survived. It didn't really matter that Hardy didn't want to be with her. It was just that she had never felt a rivalry in love before. It was she who could always decide if she didn't want to be with someone. Maybe she should seek a relationship that had more stability, she considered. One with less physical attraction and one she could harmonize with spiritually.

As Emmy rolled off her bed, the metal frame creaked. She stood up slowly, then walked to her desk and dipped a pen in a jar of ink.

"Dear Mr. Ball," she wrote in formal penmanship. "I wanted to tell you I have no more toothache…"

She wrote the note hurriedly and to the point, informing Hugo that she had something to tell him and asking if he could meet her. Then, she signed the letter and ran it to the post, praying he would receive it before he left Munich.

***

Emmy walked along the sidewalk that led to Café Luitpold. The marble columns along the covered sidewalk illuminated her steps like a film strip. She moved quietly along the path that transitioned from dark to light, appearing from behind the shadows as if she were in a silent movie.

The café was in a grand building with more than 20 halls. A painted domed ceiling gave it the appearance of a castle, and it was always packed with people who were happy being social – even during the war.

As she turned the corner toward the entrance, she nearly stumbled back as she found herself face-to-face with the man she hoped to meet.

"You said it was urgent," Hugo said, holding the letter in his hand. He opened the door for her and allowed her to go in.

"Hugo," she said, trying to conjure up her feelings. Now that he was there, she wasn't sure what she wanted to say. Maybe it was a mistake to meet him. Did she want to be with him? "Mr. Ball," she said, remaining formal. "Please, I'd like to know your opinion on a specific matter."

"Okay," he said. "What is it?"

Emmy shuffled in her chair. "Well... it's about something I read once from Nietzsche."

"Nietzsche?" Hugo asked.

"Well, yes," she said. Not knowing exactly how to explain. "You're familiar with his writing, aren't you?"

"Yes," he confirmed. "I studied him in school."

"Well..." Emmy said. "He says that a friendship between a man and woman cannot exist unless there is a mutual physical aversion to the other."

"That's what you called me here to talk about?" He looked disappointed. "Why are you asking me this?"

"I don't know," she said, suddenly embarrassed. "I guess it is not always possible to tell so accurately why someone is dealing with a question."

"Well," Hugo replied after some thought. "I supposed it must be true."

She looked at him, hoping he'd say something else.

"I mean, it probably is true what Nietzsche says. But, of course, there can be exceptions. In some cases, I'm sure it could work."

"Really?" Emmy asked. "Might you consider it?"

He paused for a moment. "I suppose I can try."

Hugo smiled, and suddenly Emmy saw that look that drew her in. His eyes, deep with an intelligent, mysterious expression.

"I would, too," she said, smiling.

The sound of wine glasses clattering broke the silence as a waiter cleared the table beside them. They talked until the music stopped playing and the lights turned on. Then, Hugo stood up and helped Emmy with her coat.

"I'm leaving Munich in a few days," he said as they walked outside. "If you happen to find yourself in Berlin, feel free to look me up."

Emmy looked at Hugo, who was silhouetted by a streetlamp. The air was mild and warm, and a silent, silver sky surrounded them. The moon above illuminated their bodies in a gold glow. And, in a moment that she wished had lasted an eternity, she kissed Hugo goodbye, raising up on her tiptoes.

10

Riot in the Street

When Emmy woke up the next morning, she decided to go to church. Maybe there, she thought, she would find something to believe in. She was still a little unsettled by Hardy's engagement, but leaving Hugo in the middle of the street didn't make her feel good either.

She put on a silk dress with a floral print, a wool coat, and a French beret. She couldn't often decide what it was that she wanted, except when it came to what to wear.

As she walked out of her apartment, Emmy breathed in the fresh air. It was cool and crisp but lacked the saltiness of her childhood hometown. She missed the seaside sometimes – the little port town on the border of Germany and Denmark where she was from. Where they greeted each other with a "*moin moin*," for "hello" and "goodbye," but it could also mean "beautiful" and "good." She remembered how, as children, they would dare each other to run across the low fog that blanketed the sea. Sometimes she still dreamed she could walk on water, but knew it was a special feat reserved only for saints.

Emmy hadn't been to church for at least three years after the nuns told her they were unable to help care for Annemarie. That was when she decided to bring her daughter home to her mother. The city was no place for a child, Emmy's mother had told her. The countryside was better for the little girl to grow up.

Emmy had considered joining a covenant prior to that, but she changed her mind after Erich, rather rudely, reminded her of the celibacy. "Who will sprinkle your little garden?" he had asked her once. Emmy almost broke up with him after that.

She hadn't known God growing up. She didn't go to church or regularly pray. To her, heaven was simply everything beyond the sea. As a child, she dreamed of working as a stewardess who would fly to Sumatra or a chambermaid on a farm in South Africa. She even considered working as a nanny in India. But when she turned 15 and left home to find work, the only work she was offered was cleaning hotel rooms.

Emmy was never good at housekeeping, so a few weeks later, she quit. Then, she found a job at a photo studio, developing prints. It was there where she slept in the attic with three other girls when Emmy started dreaming and envisioning her fairytale ending.

***

Emmy pulled her jacket closer to her body as she got closer to the city center. She remembered how the sailors would come into the port and sing drunken songs on their way home from the bar. How she had watched them from the attic windows, dreaming that they might fall in love with her. A woman could travel anywhere with a man at her side: Batavia, Budapest, Paris, Munich, Zurich, or Rome. Alone, though, even walks and bicycle rides could be dangerous, especially after a certain time of night.

As Emmy made her way to Ludwigskirche, she turned down Amalienstrasse. The Simplicisimus was nearby, just a few blocks up from Café Luitpold. She thought about what she had proposed to Hugo at the café. She wondered if the best way forward really was to just be friends or if she had underestimated how much she needed him.

She thought about the patterns in her past relationships. Her first husband, her daughter's father, Hardy, Erich... and whether they had ended because she or they had been wrong. And now, whether she was truly lonely or if it was just because the weather was cold.

When Emmy reached the square across from the church, there was a crowd of people in front of a newspaper stand where a newsboy was shouting about a war victory. "Germany and Turkey defeat the Russian Navy in the Black Sea!"

"Spread the news," another boy said. He didn't look much older than ten. He handed her a postcard of Kaiser Wilhelm II, with his full mustache pointed sharply upward, sitting on a horse like an apocalyptic Sunday rider.

The German Emperor, whom Emmy had met once as a child, had recently declared the end of multiple political parties in Germany. As far as he was concerned, there was only one German; he told reporters. Two years prior, he had been nominated for a Nobel Peace Prize, and that summer, *The New York Times* called him a "hero of peace."

Emmy thought he looked grumpy in the photo and wondered how it was possible that he was doing better in business than she was. If it were her photos being handed out in the street, people would be singing and dancing instead of fighting and grieving.

Emmy put the postcard in her pocket, then turned a corner toward the church's marble spires. The morning sun bathed them in a warm autumn light. As she walked toward her sanctuary, she passed a few old stone houses. One painted a welcoming yellow specifically caught her eye.

Emmy took a step back to admire the home, then realized there was something written on the wall. In thick white chalk scrawled across the facade: THERE ARE STILL WAR BONDS TO BE BOUGHT!

Emmy tried to make sense of the message, but as she was reading, an old man came outside of the home. She watched as the man read the message, then went back inside and slammed the door.

A few seconds later, the man returned with a bucket and rag in his hand. Emmy watched from across the street as he wiped away the words. Then he pulled out a piece of chalk and wrote: BLESSED ARE THE PEACEMAKERS, FOR THEY WILL POSSESS THE EARTH!!!

By the time the old man had finished the third exclamation mark, a crowd of people had gathered around her. Emmy hadn't even noticed the others until someone started to yell profanities.

"We've been attacked, you old git!"

Then, before she knew what was happening, another man from the crowd punched the old man in the face. Blood ran from his nose and onto his white shirt. A younger man stood over him, continuing to yell at him.

"Is that the answer you asked Christ for?" the younger man said. "Someone who doesn't want to fight? You want us to all sit back and watch our country fall? Allow France, Russia, and England to grow more powerful than us? Germany is our fatherland. Is it not yours?"

"The old man is crazy," someone else yelled from the crowd. "Leave him alone."

"No," the old man said as drops of bright red blood fell from his nose. "I'm not crazy. This is a fight for and against peace."

Emmy considered walking away, but then she remembered the postcard of the Kaiser she had in her pocket. There might have been a war victory that morning, but it was obvious the news was not bringing harmony. She wished the Kaiser could see all the fear he was inciting. From the postcards to the street to the crowd surrounding her. There was a demand to be patriotic or face a battle on their own land. If you weren't a nationalist, then you were against your homeland.

There hadn't been a real war in Europe in more than 40 years. However, there had always been disputes amongst the neighbors. Germany and France were always at odds, and the German elite looked down at Russia, which had allied with England in 1907.

Emmy looked at the 70-something-year-old child of God who was facing death for writing words of peace on his wall. His blood, as bright as a rose in the surrounding world of gray.

"Here!" Emmy yelled into the crowd. "Look!" She held up the postcard photo of the Kaiser.

"We may have been attacked, but one cannot use peace as propaganda," she said. "Wake up! Let's not be so sentimental."

Emmy heard the sound of the slap first. Then, she felt a burning sensation rising from her face. Someone had hit her on her right cheek.

"Hit me!" Emmy cried, holding her hand up to the pain. "Hit me again. I want to go back to sleep."

Quickly a brawl began to grow. Everyone started pushing and shoving. Dust and slurs flew up from the cobblestone road.

"What is all this commotion?" A man in uniform blew a whistle and made his way to the center of the crowd.

"It's high treason," Emmy said. "You don't need to know the details, but no matter how Germany acts, at least the world must be shaped by peacemakers."

The officer wasn't even looking at her. "Everyone, get out of here." He blew his whistle again.

"We have already left each other in our hearts," Emmy yelled back at him. She could feel her eye swelling. She turned away, but before she took a step, five strong fingers grasped her arm and spun her back around.

"I could arrest you," the officer warned. "I mean it. Don't upset me."

Upset? She thought. She was upset enough that things were so unfair in this world. But how could she explain this to an officer who was used to having blood on his hands.

Emmy looked at his hand, gripping her arm, then she started to wail loudly, like a child.

She didn't know why her tears fell so fully. Maybe it was the suggestion of prison, or maybe, she thought, she was suffering for the old man.

As she gasped for air, the officer let go of her arm, leaving her with her tears streaming down her swollen cheek. Emmy was still crying as the officer left her and went over to the old man, who was lying on the ground. She watched him help the man up. Then, she pushed her way out of the crowd, holding her cheek and her head down toward the ground.

She turned the corner to go back home, the blood and tears running down her lips. It tasted of iron and salt. Where was God now?

"Emmy?" A voice called out beside her.

Emmy looked over her shoulder but didn't see anyone. Then, she looked in the other direction and found herself in an Oriental dream. A woman with a colorful scarf draped around her head stood beside her, like a mirage, an illusion in a desert.

"Emmy, dear, why are you crying?"

She wasn't dreaming, Emmy realized. It was really Else. She hadn't seen her since the night backstage at the Simplicissimus. She looked at her friend, and before she could say anything, Else wrapped her arm around her and led her into a café.

11

Japonisme

"One apple pie, please," Else told the waiter. "With whipped cream. Also, a napkin, please, and a bowl of water."

The scarf draped around Else's head accentuated her big brown eyes and rounded cheeks. She looked at Emmy warmly but with a sense of concern.

"We should get you a patch for your eye, dear," she said. "It will help with the swelling."

"No," Emmy replied, turning away from her. "I'm fine. Besides, I'll probably get beaten again today or tomorrow."

Emmy didn't see who had hit her, but it didn't matter anyway. The air had had a collective feeling of hatred fueled by the inhumanity of war.

The waiter returned quickly with the bowl of water, and Else pulled out a small bottle of antiseptic from her purse. Then she dipped the napkin in the liquid and placed it on Emmy's cheek.

"Please, Else," Emmy said, pushing away her friend's hand. "I have to see the world. One must be able to see through the pain to see what is going on these days."

Else smiled sadly back at her. She looked graceful in her turban, which covered most of her curly hair. But then, Emmy noticed that the colors of the scarf were black, red, and gold, just like the German flag.

"Jesus, Else," Emmy exclaimed. "Are you so self-righteous that you wear flags in the middle of the day?"

"I prefer to be referred to as the *Prince of Thebes*," replied Else. "I may have entered this world as a German, but I was born in Egypt. And I am Jewish, Emmy, if you remember. People mistake me all the time for a foreigner. What if someone thinks I'm a spy? You have to learn how to survive in a foreign country without forgetting where you came from."

Emmy didn't know how to reply. A spy? Was that not just a role in a play? She knew Else liked to act as characters from different cultures, but she wasn't sure why she suddenly felt the need to be so *German*.

"Look," Else said, pulling another scarf from her bag. "I even bought a blue and white one to represent Bavaria."

Else held up the scarf between her and Emmy. "How do you like it? It's a bit more discreet than the one I'm wearing, right?"

"Chic," Emmy said, even though she didn't believe it. She used her hand to gently pull the curtain down between them. "But, believe me, Else. We have not been attacked. It's just that we are not allowed to suggest anything different."

Suddenly, the café got quiet. Else sat up straighter, and everyone stopped talking. Emmy had meant to voice her opinion discreetly, but now, she realized, nearly everyone was listening.

"Your pie," the waiter said, giving Emmy a stern look. He slammed the plate down in front of her, spilling whipped cream off the side of it.

Emmy handed the man the water bowl. "Here," she said in the same tone as his. "We're done with this."

"Emmy," Else said gently, in a way to urge her to calm down, but Emmy was too upset to worry about anyone else.

"You read the news, Else. You see the mixed messages in the papers. One day, the Japanese are our friends, and the next day, they're our enemy. The news articles refer to them as a 'fine yellow race' one day and 'stinking monkeys' the next. And must we accept it?"

"What else can we do?" Else asked. "Everyone has their alliances. If Japan decides to go to war over their allegiance with England, then they will discover themselves what their fate is."

Emmy looked at her sadly, "Tell Toulouse-Lautrec or Vincent Van Gogh that they can no longer be inspired by Japan. One cannot just hate what they have loved from one day to the next."

12

Responsible

As the war went on, Emmy realized just how much it affected everyone around her. Families lost their fathers, sons left home to fight, food became scarce, and the wealthy withdrew all their cash from the banks.

Emmy tried to stay positive while maintaining her stance against the war. She and Else even attended peace rallies, where they reunited with Lottie, who was passing out signs with anti-war slogans.

Just as Else had suggested when she had hidden behind her scarf, anything construed as being foreign was now forbidden. There was even a "Committee for Good German Advertising Language," established by the government so that no foreign words would be used for what could be said in German.

Across the country, it was no longer correct to say the French *"Adieu,"* when parting; only the formal German, *"Auf Widersehen,"* was permitted. Café Windsor became *Kaffee Winzer,* Piccadilly Café became *Kaffeehaus Vaterland,* and the Hotel Bristol simply went without a name. Even the American cigarettes "Dandy" and "Gibson Girl" were renamed *"Dalli"* and *"Pennant."*

Emmy couldn't stand the nationalism, especially after seeing innocent people get hurt in the street. And even though she had told Kathi she could sing the patriotic songs, she never could.

She spent her days quietly, mostly at home. Sometimes, she would sing on the street to earn enough to buy dinner. She worried she would have to start entertaining men, but then Lottie said she could get Emmy a job as a seamstress.

***

"I'll never be any good at this," Emmy said, throwing the uniform onto the floor. Its color was called *"feldgrau,"* which was a dull, greenish gray.

She looked over at Lottie, who was sewing at a table next to her. Rows of women, two-by-two, were at the machines that filled the room.

"Don't worry," Lottie said, smiling. "You'll get better at it."

"I'm not so sure," Emmy said.

Emmy was glad she had been reunited with Lottie. When she had seen her at the peace rally, she had jumped into her arms and kissed her. That had made the men around them go wild and whistle, but Emmy had just rolled her eyes and held her tight.

Since that day, she and Lottie had practically been inseparable. Sewing day-in and day-out at a small factory just outside the city. Emmy had thought the job would be easier. But she learned quickly that while she could make a peasant blouse out of trousers or a rococo costume from furniture trim, she wasn't as precise with her sewing as she wished.

Emmy watched Lottie as she pulled a thread through a needle, slipped it through a button, and tied a knot with her teeth. Lottie reminded Emmy of the fairytale princess Snow White. She worked steadfastly and passionately with everything she did, with the careful look of a young deer, yet so full of trust.

"I don't know about you, but I think it's about time to get out of here." Emmy looked over at the woman talking at the table next to them.

"Leave Germany?" Another woman responded back to her. "And how exactly are you going to do that? You think they'll let you cross the border when your husband is at war?"

Emmy stayed silent, pretending to focus on her sewing as she listened in to the women's conversation.

"He's coming home for Christmas," the woman said. "I know a friend who can get us a passport."

Then Emmy had an idea. If she could get a passport, maybe she could get some freedom back.

"Lottie," Emmy said, looking over at her friend. "Do you think it's selfish to want to love when the world is full of hate?"

Lottie thought for a few seconds, then said, "Love is something we need as much as eating or breathing."

Emmy nodded. "It just seems like, with this war, there's more of an importance placed in fighting for this country instead of for our own dreams. We're lucky, in a way, aren't we, that we don't have to go to the front like the men? But sometimes I feel like I'm suffering just as much as they are."

Lottie agreed. "I know," she said. "It's not easy for anyone."

"So, what do we do?"

"I don't know," Lottie said. "Keep busy. Find a way to escape."

"Yeah," Emmy said. "But how?"

"Well…" Lottie looked around to see if anyone was listening. "Don't tell anyone, but Gerhard sometimes gets me a prescription that helps." She pulled a small glass bottle from her purse and tossed it toward Emmy. "I tell him it's for my cramps."

Emmy caught the bottle in the air. She had forgotten that Lottie's fiancé was a doctor. She twisted open the cap and took a sip of the Heroin.

"Thanks," Emmy said. "I needed that."

"Keep it," she said. "I can get a new one. It's almost that time of the month." She winked.

For the next few hours, they continued their work, talking about life and how they were learning to cope. All the while, Emmy still considered asking the woman next to her about the passports. Lottie told Emmy how she, too, had fallen into a state of uncertainty since the war began and how, now that the theaters had changed, she had less work as a costume designer. What she really wanted to do, she told Emmy, was make dolls.

"Like puppets?" Emmy asked.

"Yes, but more delicate," Lottie said. "Actually," she reached under the desk for her purse and pulled out a wax figure.

Emmy gently took the doll from her hands. It had short black hair, just like her maker, but her body was thinner and elongated.

"I was hoping to sew her a little dress with leftover fabric, but I'm not sure *feldgrau* is her color.

"Do you make them so delicate on purpose?" Emmy asked, looking at the little wax fingers. Their eyes were large, and they had pouted lips.

"Well, not at first," she said, "but I suppose, in a way, they do represent the fragile nature of childhood."

Emmy took another look at the doll's thin legs and oversized head. They were not made for children to play with.

"They're almost erotic, aren't they?" Emmy asked, touching the tiny wax toes.

"Ha," Lottie giggled. "I guess I hadn't really thought of it. Though, I suppose neither of us can suppress decadence, can we." She smiled at her.

"I know I need to find a new outlet for my energy soon," Emmy said. "If I can't sing or love, then what's the point of living?" Suddenly, she felt the morphine kick in. She handed the doll back to Lottie, who placed the doll carefully back in her bag.

"I think I'm going to call it a night," Emmy said. The shift bell had rang, and other women had started packing.

"I'll see you tomorrow," Lottie said. "I'm just going to finish a few more shirts." She leaned over and kissed Emmy's cheeks. "Get home safe."

***

It was already dark by the time Emmy got outside, but the sky was filled with stars, and there was not a cloud in sight. Emmy looked up and admired the sparkling lights, remembering that she, too, was just a tiny doll in the big expanse of the universe. Still, she chose the brightest star she could find and wished upon it for herself.

When she arrived at her apartment, Emmy checked her mail. She pulled out a stack of letters and shuffled them through her hands. There was a pamphlet – some propaganda for war – a note from her landlord and a letter with no stamp.

She stared at the letter, which was formal and crisp, then realized it must be from the government. Their correspondence was free to deliver, unlike more important correspondence, such as urgent love letters.

Emmy slid her finger under the seal and read the letter in the moonlight. It was a subpoena for court, she realized, for the undisclosed charges against her.

Emmy stood outside for a few minutes, thinking about what to do, then went into her home and tossed the subpoena on the table. The morphine made her dizzy, but it also helped calm her nerves. She didn't want to imagine going back to prison, so she would try to forget it. Anyway, she didn't even know how she could defend herself.

She looked around her room for signs of comfort: her bed, a small table, two wooden chairs, photos of saints on her walls, dried roses, and paintings by her friends. She lit a couple of candles and placed them around her room. Then, she reached into her coat pocket and took another sip of the Heroin.

Whatever there was to worry about, she thought, she would worry about it later.

13

Wild, or Free

Emmy gasped in fear, and her eyes shot open. She had been dreaming of a summer's day, but a loud noise woke her up. She stayed in bed and looked out the window, through which warm rays of sunshine fell on her body.

At first, Emmy thought the noise was in her head, but then she heard it again. Someone was knocking. She tried to think who it could be.

"One minute!" Emmy called as she threw on a sweater and a pair of socks from the floor. She looked at herself in the mirror. Her hair was a mess. The knocking was getting louder.

Emmy smiled as she opened the door, but the man on the other side didn't look happy.

"*Guten Morgen*," he said in formal German. He had a wide nose and burly arms that were covered in dark hair. "Are you Frau Hennings?"

Fräuline, Emmy thought. She was single, divorced, but still used her married name. She was a *Frau*, yes, but not an old woman like her mother. Yet, there was no other term for a young, divorced woman in German.

"Yes," she said, slightly apprehensively. "I'm her."

"You were to have received a letter requesting your presence at trial." The man stepped into her apartment, causing Emmy to stumble backward.

She looked at him, confused at first, then noticed the silver badge on his chest and remembered the subpoena. She looked over to the table. It was covered with her poems, photos of her at the cabaret, and half-written letters to her mother.

"Oh, yes," she said, picking up a vase of wilting roses. She rummaged through the papers. "I believe it only just came in the mail last night. I didn't have a chance to read it…"

The officer pushed open her door wider and walked into her home. His boots left muddy footprints on her floor.

"Here it is," Emmy said. "I've found it." She held up the letter as the officer walked over next to her.

"Am I being arrested?" she asked, taking a step back. "I don't need an escort. I can make it to the courthouse. I'm innocent anyway."

"That's not up for you to say," the officer responded aggressively.

"Please tell me, sir, if I am being arrested." Emmy was growing more nervous. "I have the right to know."

The officer didn't say anything in return; instead, his attention was focused on the photos on the table. The ones Emmy sold between acts and after shows, which showed her in a red dress on the cabaret stage.

Emmy looked at the officer, then at herself. She closed her eyes and inhaled deeply, trying to figure out what to do next.

"It doesn't help me not to know what I'm being accused of," Emmy said. "How can someone judge me if I cannot judge myself?"

"Frau Hennings," the man said, his voice growing sterner. "You need to come with me."

"But," she said. "I'm hardly ready. Can you come back this afternoon?"

She looked at the clock. It was already 1:30.

"Do you want to join me now, Mrs. Hennings, or would you prefer you're brought there by force?"

Emmy thought about what she needed to do. Her mind was still in a haze from the medicine. She grabbed her purse and nicest coat and put on her beloved French beret.

"Ok," she said. She looked at the man sadly. "I think I'm ready."

As Emmy stepped outside, she crossed herself in prayer, leaving just a few steps between the officer and herself. Thankfully, the sun was shining, and there were signs of spring. Fresh, yellow-green buds graced the trees.

"How free is the air," she said. "How cute and how wild."

The officer didn't say anything. His handcuffs gently swayed from his back pocket.

"It's as if it sends promises of love," she continued, despite his silent protest. "A love that could burn so bright it would last until the rainy season was done."

14

Erich

Emmy ran out of the courthouse and started to cry. She was all alone despite all the people nearby. No one paid any attention to her as tears flowed down her face. As she crossed the street and made her way through the alleys, no one smiled and said *"Guten Tag"* or "Good day."

It would be much nicer, Emmy thought if more people saw life eye-to-eye. She wished someone would reach out to her and ask her how she was doing. She had felt an air of optimism on the way to the courthouse, but after receiving her sentence, she was beginning to lose faith again.

When she got back to her apartment, she went straight to her bed, burying her face in the pillows.

How could it be that one could be found guilty despite their innocence? And whose right was it to convict her besides herself and her maker?

Emmy was still crying when there was a knock on her door. She held her breath in her chest and hoped it was in error. She used to believe every knock was an opportunity, but after all she had been through, she was scared to answer.

After another knock, a man's voice called out from behind the door.

"Emmy? Are you home?"

She thought she'd recognized the voice, which was enough to get her out of bed. And when she opened the door, she saw to her delight that it was Erich.

Emmy threw her arms around her friend and pressed her face into his shoulder.

"Emmy," Erich said with a sound of relief. "It's been a while."

Emmy looked up at Erich and smiled. His face was thinner, and he was growing a beard, but he still had the same full head of shaggy hair.

"Where have you been?" Erich asked, stepping inside her apartment. "I haven't seen you lately at the café. Are you buying your own coffee these days?"

Emmy gave him an innocent look. He always had something to mock her about. "I suppose life has just been playing out differently lately," she said. "What are you doing here? Would you like some tea?"

"I was just in the neighborhood," he said. "Sure, thank you."

Emmy offered him a seat at the table and then went to the small gas cookstove to boil water.

"So…" he said, looking around her room. "How have you been, Emmy?"

"Not great, really," she said. "I just got back from court, actually."

"Court? Why? What did you do now?"

"I didn't do anything!" Emmy exclaimed. "I'm innocent." She threw up her hands, almost knocking over the pot of boiling water. Erich stood up quickly to save her, but a little water just swirled out of the pot and settled back again.

"Be careful," he said, placing a hand on her shoulder. Emmy turned into his chest and started crying again.

"I haven't done anything wrong," she said. "I've been falsely accused. The real problem is that I'm a woman in a world ruled by men, which prevents me from even having a say."

Eric looked at her critically. "Well, that's probably true," he said, "but what do they accuse you of?"

"I don't know," Emmy said. "I received a letter a few days ago, and then today, an officer showed up at my door escorting me to the courthouse. They accuse me of theft, for stealing a watch, but the man whose watch I allegedly stole wasn't even there to accuse me."

Emmy placed a mug of steaming black tea in front of Erich. "Sorry," she said. "I don't have any milk."

"It's fine," he said. They both stayed quiet, watching the steam. "But why would they say you stole if you didn't."

Emmy gave Erich a little more detail. About how hard life had been and how she couldn't sing or make money. How sometimes she would go home with random men.

"Oh, well, that makes sense, doesn't it?" Erich said. Emmy could tell he was judging her. "Whether or not you're guilty won't matter then, will it? Once you're on their list of those who live on the fringe of society, you'll forever be a target."

Emmy wondered if that was true.

"Did they give you a sentence?" he asked, adjusting his thin-rimmed glasses on his face.

"Three weeks in prison," she said.

"For stealing a watch?"

"I didn't steal it!" she said, emphasizing her innocence. "Still, they make me responsible. Does that mean I am?"

"Did you refute it?"

"I tried," she said, feeling like she might cry again. "I listened to the accusations, but I was in shock. I could only shake my head and remain silent."

"Oh, Emmy," Erich said. He almost looked like he felt bad for her. "You'll survive. Three weeks isn't too bad. Did I ever tell you about the boarding school I went to as a child? That place was way worse than prison."

Emmy shook her head.

"I was a good writer growing up. I wanted to be a poet, but my father was insistent I study pharmaceuticals. He put me in a boarding school that was known for its authoritarian punishment, knowing full well any individual dream I had would be beaten out of me. The writer, Thomas Mann, actually attended the same school and wrote about how terrible the teachers there were in his first novel."

Emmy listened intently. She had known that he wanted to be a poet, but that was about the extent of it.

"Anyway," he said. "By the time I was 16, I was tired of all the whips of a birch tree branch across my knuckles and back. So, I wrote an anonymous opinion piece about how terrible the school was and published it in the newspaper. I suggested the community start a petition to expel a specifically cruel teacher, which created quite a scandal. At first, no one knew who would incite such a public aspersion, but when they found out it was me, I was expelled for 'participating in socialist activities.'"

Emmy looked at Erich sadly, allowing him time to reach the moral of his story.

"Maybe you are right," he said. "About how men and women are treated differently. Not just with language and law but with all of society's expectations. Maybe it doesn't have to be a bad thing. Maybe everything that is put in our path only invokes more resilience."

"Still," he said, holding her hand tightly across the table. "One must be careful with how they live these days."

15

Passport Factory

Emmy served her three-week sentence, which was similar to the first. Lonely, depressing, cold and stressful. Her basic needs of food, water, and shelter were barely being met, yet Emmy stayed emotionally detached enough to be resilient, like Erich said.

But then, just as Erich could have predicted, as soon as she got out of jail, she was put back in again. This time, though, she wasn't in a normal prison. She was under protective military custody, along with another woman.

The woman, Margot, was the one who sat next to her at the factory. Emmy had finally gained the courage to ask her about the passports. Margot had told her that she could get her some papers, but that she had to go with her to the immigration office to apply for them.

Emmy didn't know why she even needed a passport. Just a few months ago, traveling across Europe was borderless. No one asked why someone was somewhere or who someone was when they got there. She loved the anonymity of travel, which allowed her to be anyone she wanted – from a Parisian shopkeeper in Moscow to a Moskvichkian butcher in Paris.

Now, though, because of the war, Germany, Italy, and France were all requiring proof of citizenship when traveling. It was a way, the news reported, to secure borders and control citizens.

***

Emmy looked over at Margot, who was visibly shaking. She hadn't said one word to Emmy since they had been arrested.

"Hennings!" An officer called out her name and opened the barred gate. He led her over to a desk where she could use the phone. Emmy didn't have to think long about who she should call. She only had one emergency contact left in the city, and even though she knew he would be upset, she called Erich.

"My God, Emmy, what did you do now?" Eric asked as soon as the operator transferred the call.

"Nothing," she said. "They think we run a fake passport factory." She couldn't even understand what she was saying even though she was saying it. She didn't even know what a passport looked like, let alone how to make one.

Erich was quiet on the other side of the line. I don't know, Emmy. If you're not telling the truth..."

"I am," she said. "I swear to God."

"...because if you're not, I will put you in a mental institution. Do you hear me? I will phone up Doctor Baron von Schrenck-Notzing and have him diagnose your kleptomaniac disposition."

"Erich," Emmy said, trying to get through to him. "Please, can you just help me get out of here?"

"I don't know," he said. "I'll see what I can do."

"Thank you," she said. Then, he hung up.

Emmy looked down at the phone, which was making a loud disconnected sound. Even though he had threatened it, Emmy knew Erich would never let her down.

She looked over at the officer who was monitoring her call. He had warm, brown eyes and seemed to be around her age. In fact, he reminded her a little of a lion tamer whom she had performed with in Gdansk. She smiled at him, trying to elicit a response of empathy or maybe, lust.

"I'm not guilty," she said after the man didn't return her affection. "I wouldn't even know how to forge a passport if I tried."

"I'm sure," he replied with no emotion to his voice. "What is it that you do then, Frau Hennings?"

"Oh," Emmy thought about it for a moment. She had chosen some desperate measures to make a living lately. "Various things…" she replied. "I sing, and I write."

"Well, then," he said, "You must have a typewriter and a photo of yourself?"

"Well, yes," Emmy said. "I type all my poems."

"So, that's all you need to make a passport."

She looked into his eyes again, trying to tell if he was serious, but they seemed somehow colder now than they were before. With a wave of his arm he led her back to the cell, then shut the door behind him and turned the lock.

16

An Uncomfortable Dream

It was during this time when Emmy wasn't sure how she would survive the day. Everything was more uncertain than ever, even more so than before. Through all the highs and lows, this was one of the worst. She spent every day in solitude, and everything was quiet.

The last thing Emmy remembered was trying to sing. She had been standing at the window, her voice directed toward heaven. But as soon as the words left her mouth, they didn't make any sense. Then everything got dark, and her head hit the floor.

The same thing happened after her first marriage when she was 18. And again after the birth of her son and when her husband left her. She wanted to call her mother but knew that she couldn't. Not because the warden wouldn't let her use the phone but because her mother would disown her.

She had already put her mother through enough, she thought, once she regained consciousness. She had left her to raise her children, even *if* that's what her mother had wanted. She was a conservative woman and believed the traditional way was the only way one should proceed in life. In her eyes, being an actress was the same thing as being a Gypsy.

When Emmy would get sick as a child, her mother would try to distract her by telling her how much sicker other people were. She recounted stories from the Bible about leprosy and tuberculosis, trying to diminish the severity of her illness. Often, it was just a stomachache or growing pains that afflicted young Emmy, but when her mother told her about the other symptoms, she could imagine herself developing them as well.

After the divorce from her first husband, the father of her son, Emmy, fell into an illness worse than she ever had before. It started as an ear infection, then turned into chills, followed by fatigue, and a high fever. The doctor told her it was depression and suggested she move cities and imagine a new start.

Emmy had suffered greatly during that time, trying to decide how to manage her future. She was only 19 and had just gotten her start as a performer. She wanted to join a theater company and become a famous singer, but instead, she was living with her mother and raising a sick little baby.

She complained to her mother, who had taken the role of the primary caretaker of her child and who was always busy coddling the baby instead of her. Each day that passed, Emmy fell more ill. Her hearing tightened, and her ears became clairaudient. She had tried to surrender herself beyond her negative thoughts, but the ringing in her ears prevented her from hearing her highest self. If there was only a way to make sense of the worries in her head, she had thought at the time, then there would be no need for faith, just the confidence of knowing.

Even now, lying on the cold cement floor of the prison, Emmy believed that humans had the power to master their natural instincts – if they could endure the sensuality along with the spirituality. This had led her to believe that it was her husband's atheist qualities that had really come between them. His moral values didn't line up with hers. She had also learned he had been kissing a shopgirl.

Emmy thought about saints a lot during their divorce, but even women whom she could look up to, like Eve or the Virgin Mary, were known for their sexual behaviors. Emmy recalled their stories cautiously, knowing they were written by men, who were, in her opinion, plagued with anxiety about the female form. They had taken Eve, for example, the most natural being, and transformed her into a temptress to teach shame and morality. And Mary, simple and pure, was designed to set impossible standards for virginity and motherhood. It was a shame, she thought, that neither woman was allowed any room in their identities to present a positive role of their sexuality.

Thus, Emmy vowed to avoid the role of the religious woman, despite the disapproval of her pious mother. Instead, she decided she would do what made her happy. That's when she made the choice to join a troupe of actors and leave her son behind with his grandmother.

Emmy remembered how she felt when she learned her son had died. He had been a small baby at birth and suffered from a long bout of whooping cough. Her mother was adamant that the sea air would do the child good, but one day, the baby fell asleep in his grandmother's arms and didn't wake up.

Emmy had blamed herself for God taking the innocent child. Then, she remembered the story of Saint Cecilia, who had sang her heart to the Lord. And so, every time Emmy sang after that, she prayed that his youth would stay forever.

***

"Get up!" a man's voice yelled at her from between the bars. Emmy could feel a cold presence behind her.

"Please," Emmy cried. "Let me be." It was dark in her cell, and she was alone.

"Why are you on the floor?"

Emmy heard him but didn't have the strength to explain.

"I can't move," she said in a somewhat lost, tender voice. "It's like my wings have been clipped. My legs feel as heavy as stone Roman columns."

Emmy heard the man grumble, then the sound of a key in a lock. The warden stepped into the room, allowing light from the hall to shine in. It warmed and brightened her vision as she lay on the cement ground in a fetal position.

"Get up," he said. "Get off the floor."

Emmy looked up at him. It was the same officer as before. The one with piercing gray eyes and a strong, lean stance.

"I can't," Emmy cried. "I can't move my body."

"What do you mean?" he said. "Do you need to see a doctor?"

Emmy started to cry, her tears pooling onto the cold tiles. Then, without saying a word, he left her there and locked the door.

***

"Conversion neurosis," the doctor said. Emmy wondered if Erich had ordered the physician. He had threatened to send her to a mental institution, and this doctor seemed to lack empathy.

"It's a form of hysteria," he told her. "A result of shifting energy."

Emmy did believe him, though. Her energy had been wildly unpredictable lately.

"Do you have any unresolved conflicts?" he asked.

"Of course," Emmy said. "Don't we all?" She didn't really want to recount all her sins again.

"The drug withdrawals aren't helping either," the doctor said, taking her pulse with his fingers. "What are you taking? Morphine?"

Emmy didn't like how he made such assumptions. A judgment on character was not necessary in such a situation in which he was already the superior.

"I have a prescription for Heroin" she said.

It wasn't the drugs, though, Emmy thought. She had her own theory for her illness. The only thing that ever cured her pains in the past was by freeing herself of the restrictions placed against her. She needed to find a way in life that was not forced upon her.

17

The Catalyst

Emmy walked the long, narrow hall toward her cell. Her gray slippers squeaked on the freshly mopped floor. The acrid smell of detergent from the bucket she was carrying mingled with the stench of onions boiling in the kitchen.

The doctor had released her after she had some time to rest, but each day that Emmy stayed in jail, the paralysis threatened to overtake her again. She tried her best to stay hopeful, believing each day she would be freed, but alas, it was impossible for a bound prisoner to forget their prison.

Emmy finished cleaning the hall, then returned the bucket and mop to the closet behind the warden's desk. The guards had been nicer to her since the incident, offering her extra bread at dinner and even giving her books to read.

"You have a visitor," the warden told Emmy as she closed the closet door.

"A visitor?" Emmy asked. "Who?" No one had ever visited her in all the times she had been in prison. Not even her mother, who, to be fair, didn't know she was there because Emmy never told her.

Emmy followed the warden to the visitor's room, falling a few paces behind. She still lacked the energy to move through life quickly. When she got to the room, she nearly passed out again. Then, for the first time in weeks, she felt her heart beat again.

"Emmy! I came as soon as I heard." Hugo Ball stood up from a table and reached out to hug her.

"No touching!" the warden said sternly. Hugo looked surprised and took a step back.

Emmy glared at the warden and then sat next to Hugo at the table. They leaned in toward each other as much as they could get away with.

"Are you ok?" he asked. "When will you be out?"

Emmy couldn't speak nor take her eyes off of him. She still couldn't believe he was there. Hugo Ball. The last time they had talked, he told her he was leaving for Berlin – after they kissed goodbye in the moonlight, and she had suggested they just be friends.

She examined him now. He looked handsome and confident. Then, she suddenly became self-aware of how she might look to him. She had been in prison for weeks, and was wearing dirty, gray trousers. She didn't know when she would be released. Hugo was asking a question that she had no answer for. She started to cry.

"It's okay," he said, his body so far forward he was hovering out of his seat. He reached over the table for her hands. "You'll be out soon. I'm sure of it. I am also without peace knowing you are trapped in here."

Emmy tried to smile, but she could only shed more tears. She wanted to convince herself that she could believe him.

"When you do get out..." Hugo said, then suddenly withdrew his hands. The warden stepped beside them, and Hugo lowered his voice. "...you must come to Berlin."

"Berlin?" Emmy asked, unsure of what he had said. "There's nothing in Berlin for me. It's not any different than here in Munich. I've heard how people are suffering. There's no theater work there either..."

"I'm done with the theater," Hugo said with a serious but discerning look. "There's no time to play a disheartened puppet show at a time when the last of human culture is at stake."

Emmy looked into his eyes, which were deep brown and fiery.

"Look," he said after she didn't respond. "I just returned from Belgium. I've seen the war and what it's turning everyone into. I've tried to support my country and fight alongside my friends, but there was a reason I wasn't drafted. Maybe it was my health, but maybe it's really because they can see that I don't believe in it. I want to fight this war with like-minded people."

"What about your fiancé?" Emmy asked. If she remembered correctly, he was to be married to that actress in Vienna.

"Everything is over between us," he said.

"Over?" she asked.

"She doesn't agree with my stance against the war," he said.

"So, you're not getting married?"

"No," he said. "She accuses me of being a revolutionary and running away from my country."

"Well, she must be heartbroken."

"I don't think so," he admitted. "But she did write me later and asked what she could do in protest."

"And what did you tell her?" Emmy asked.

"I told her to form a community," he said. "To create new forms of art and expression to ward off the kitsch."

Emmy could see that Hugo was serious. She looked into his eyes again and smiled, noticing how the brown looked almost gold against the gray.

"You smile through it all," Hugo said as he leaned toward Emmy again. "You're so good. You remind me of a summer's day."

Just as Emmy considered reaching out for him, the warden's voice boomed from behind them, announcing the end of visiting hours. Emmy felt her heart jump, then sink again.

"I'll see you soon," he said as he stood to leave. When the warden looked away, he reached out and squeezed her hand.

There was no time left to thank him, let alone express all the emotions she suddenly felt for him.

***

That night at dinner, Emmy sat alone in the canteen. The high chatter of women's voices flooded across the long, metal tables. Her stomach was empty, but she didn't feel pain. Only a hollow sense of loneliness hovered between herself and a bowl of onion soup.

She looked into the thin broth, which reflected her appearance like a mirror. It was the first time she had seen her face since she had been arrested. She recognized the outline of her square jaw, her short, pageboy hair, and her eyes, which looked like two infinite black holes staring back at her.

She tried not to worry about others' opinions, but suddenly, it became important what Hugo had thought of her appearance. It had been such a wonderful surprise to see him. He had brought her a new joy that made her feel her heart again.

As the dinner bell rang, the women got up and began to clear their plates. Emmy returned her full bowl of soup and then asked the warden for a pen and paper. Then she sat down at a table while the rest of the women left.

At first, she didn't know what she would write, but then she remembered the famous words of Goethe, who said: "One must flirt with things that are dangerous, but hold onto a sense of higher purpose."

She wrote to Hugo, telling him how happy she was to see him and how her heart hurt with joy because he gave her hope again. She told him that she wished she could see him again, away from the prison guards, closer to him.

It was quite forward, Emmy knew, especially because she had suggested they just be friends, but she always tried to follow her heart, even if it conflicted with her mind. She had always trusted Hugo, even though she was never really sure why. From the first day they met at the Simplicissimus to the summer night in the garden, each time he had gone away, she thought there could still be something between them.

Maybe it was because he spoke about the future, or maybe it was the sincere look in his eyes. She knew that admitting such feelings were foolish for a woman stuck in prison, yet she still felt herself pulled to him more than anyone else at the moment.

"I have been completely free of morphine," she continued in her letter. She wanted him to know so he might have a better impression of her. "I have not been given anything since I have been in prison. So, now I do not need a sanatorium. At least prison was good for something."

She wondered what else she should tell him. She still didn't know if she wanted to go to Berlin, but she did know that she wouldn't have let go of his hand if he had reached hers.

The final bell rang out across the room as Emmy scrawled a final sentence onto the page. "Even though life is difficult," she wrote. "I am so looking forward to freedom."

18

Berlin

Emmy remained in prison all through the holidays, and although she had dreamed of Christmas, it came and went without her noticing. The New Year, too, arrived without cause for celebration. There were no holiday balls or studio parties to be invited to. Only war and cold weather.

There had been an unofficial "Christmas truce" among the Western Front, the newspapers reported. In the week before Christmas, French, British, and German troops were instructed to temporarily stop fighting. The men crossed the trenches to engage in friendly, seasonal greetings; they played football, sang carols, and exchanged food and tobacco. But while the soldiers were relaxed in "No Man's Land" between the front lines, the leaders of their countries were busy reconsidering strategies. And when the holiday celebrations ended, the killings began again. In the first three weeks of the new year, more than a million men were dead.

It had been nearly two months since Hugo had visited Emmy in prison. But in his absence, he had sent several letters. He had to return to Berlin, he wrote, but he told her that he left money with Erich if she wanted to join him there.

He wrote that she was like a mirror in which he could see his own beauty and that when he wrote her, it was almost as if he could still see her. Emmy was flattered by his words of admiration, but she worried slightly if it wasn't just his ego that he saw in her.

He, too, had said the holidays lacked festivities. He spent New Year's Eve at a friend's apartment in Berlin. He told her how they had protested against the ending year, shouting "Down with war!" into the silent night and how some passers-by on the sidewalks below had stopped to look up and stare. Other neighbors opened their windows and shouted, "Here's to the New Year!"

He hoped that some people would come around to his thinking, he wrote. "The war is without merit. It is barbarism with no Gods."

His next endeavor, he told her, would be a "Commemoration of the Fallen Poets." A showcase he was organizing in attempts to honor fallen writers. He explained how he could not just "sit inactively by a warm fireplace" while others were dying. He wouldn't fall for the nationalistic madness and hatred.

"Love is greater than hate," he wrote. "Understanding greater than ire, peace nobler than war. This exactly is what this unholy war should burn into our memories, more so than ever felt before."

At the end of every letter, he asked for Emmy to join him. "I want to be the man you call in your sleep," he told her. "Who gets up and leaves everything behind to follow you."

She was nervous about Hugo's offer. He seemed to be in the early days of love, like Don Quixote, going boldly on conquests without knowing the risk. It was as if he thought she was the bridge that could hold him, but Emmy wasn't sure she yet trusted her own sense of direction. Still, Hugo called for her with such certainty. Which, at the time, was a good enough reason to respond to his calls with an echo.

So, after her release in the spring, she went to Berlin.

***

Hugo put his arm around Emmy's shoulder as they watched the man on stage. His friend, Richard Huelsenbeck, was reading a poem. He wore a flat cap and had a warm, handsome face, but in his performance, he sounded angry.

"Huelsenbeck was in the barracks for months," Hugo whispered to Emmy as he continued watching his friend. "He was dismissed for neuralgia."

"Neuralgia?" Emmy asked. "What's that?"

"Some kind of nervous reaction," he said. "He describes it as pain pulsing like electricity through the nerves on his face."

Emmy grimaced as she looked at the man on the stage. There was a small crowd watching him, gathered in the basement of the University's architecture building. Hugo said he had expected a bigger audience, but the newspaper had refused to publicize the event, which, Hugo claimed, was because there was a French name among the list of the dead.

Back on the stage, Huelsenbeck's voice got louder and louder. He was quite good at public speaking, Emmy thought as she watched him switch between languages. He spoke with such emotion and drama. Aggressive but spontaneous and provocative, his voice booming like a loud heartbeat or drum.

"You see. It doesn't matter what he's saying," Hugo whispered, leaning into Emmy. "The laws of rhythm are what's important."

Emmy nodded.

"French, German, it's all the same to us," Huelsenbeck said, now practically preaching. "We don't know whether we, too, will cease to exist."

***

The next morning, Emmy woke to a symphony of taps and clatter. When she opened her eyes, she saw Hugo sitting at his typewriter.

"Sorry," Hugo said. "I didn't mean to wake you."

"That's okay," Emmy said, rubbing the sleep from her eyes and adjusting to the light. She had been dreaming that she was sitting on Hugo's lap like he was Father Christmas. She didn't remember what she asked for, but she did remember giving him a list of all the things that she desired.

Emmy looked at Hugo now as she rolled over in his bed. He was sitting across the room, balancing a cigarette between his lips. His fingers, long and thin, resumed their position, tapping away on the keyboard in a synchronized rhythm.

"What time is it?" she asked. It was dark outside, and the sun had not yet risen. As she sat up, her stomach rumbled, and she remembered they had gone to sleep without dinner again.

"Five-thirty," Hugo replied. "Go back to sleep if you can. I have to finish this article."

Along with the "Commemoration of the Fallen Poets," Hugo and Huelsenbeck had started their own journal. They called it *Die Aktion,* and its goal was to "exert a positive cultural influence as a necessary intellectual shock," he had told her. But despite Hugo claiming its aims were more stylistic than political, their first issue had been confiscated before it left the printer.

"What's the story?" Emmy asked from the bed. There were piles of newspapers next to Hugo, strewn across his desk and floor. He leaned down to pick one up, then held it up to show her.

"It's a total mess of machinery," he said with a tone of aggression that Emmy thought was inappropriate for such an early hour. "It's like the devil himself has broken loose now. Look." He shook the paper wildly. "The papers print photos of schoolboys marching gleefully into battle, then the next thing you know, they're reporting their death in masses by rapid machine guns."

He threw the paper back onto the floor and then looked dismally at Emmy.

"Emmy," he asked. "If my country is doing this, am I doing it too?"

Emmy sat up in bed and looked back at Hugo. She could see how much the war was impacting him. In just the few days she had been with him, his already thin face had gotten much slimmer, and he appeared more worn and sunken than he had ever been.

"Come," she said. "Lie down with me."

Hugo stayed at his desk for a moment, then slowly pushed himself away and came to bed. He laid down beside her, his face resting on her chest, and then Emmy wrapped herself around him, touching her lips to his forehead.

"You know," he said after a while. "A revolt in materialistic philosophy is more necessary than a revolt of the masses."

"Shhh…" Emmy whispered back to him. "Those who are good will come to their senses."

***

When Emmy and Hugo woke for the second time that day, they both seemed to be in a better condition. The sunlight poured over Hugo's bed, and they woke up bright-eyed and optimistic.

With almost a skip in his step, Hugo went toward the kitchen, pausing a moment at the piano to play a tune with one hand. Emmy found it erotic how quickly his fingers moved and how he could create such a beautiful sound out of thin air.

"I don't have any coffee," he said. "But there are carrots." He placed a kettle in the fireplace. Emmy smiled as she watched him make the broth, and after a few minutes, a sweet smell filled the small apartment.

Hugo reached up to remove two plates from the cupboard next to the chimney. Then, he placed them on a small table and served a spoonful of sauerkraut and a few slices of horse meat. Along with coffee, wheat had also become scarce, and bread was replaced with "K-Brot," made of dried potatoes, oats, barley, and pulverized straw.

Since November, the British had limited imports into Germany, preventing foods, fodder, and fertilizer from crossing the border. With nearly a third of Germany's goods coming from exports, the country quickly became dependent on local goods, which in turn was also in peril because the farmers and their horses were called to war, leaving their wives struggling to run the farms.

Emmy watched Hugo finish preparing their meal, and then she got out of bed and carefully put on her stockings, trying to avoid another tear. She smoothed out her nightgown, which plunged low on her chest and looked at herself in the mirror that stood between the door and an overflowing bookshelf.

"What's that?" she asked, pointing to something on the shelf.

"What?" Hugo asked. He removed the whistling kettle from the stove.

"It looks like a human head. Is it a real skull?"

"Oh," Hugo said. He walked next to her and picked up the object. "Yes, it's the head of a young woman."

Emmy looked at him, concerned.

"I found it when I was a child near the grounds of an old chapel that was being excavated," he said. "The crew said I could keep it and that she probably died in the early 1800s."

Emmy looked at the skull, which was painted colorfully. The cheekbones were covered in bright flowers like forget-me-nots and roses – the same flowers that lovers and mothers placed in the gun barrels when their men left for war.

Hugo gently picked up the skull and held it up to his face, which reminded her of a Shakespeare play. He looked fondly into the remains of the 100-year-old girl, then placed her back on the bookshelf between novels and manuscripts.

Emmy ran her finger across the titles of the books. There were mostly works by Russian philosophers. Nietzsche, Kant, Bakunin and Merezhkovsky. They were all proponents of decentralized communist societies, she realized, against central governments and for self-governing communities.

"You know Nietzsche, right?" Hugo asked. He pulled one of the books from the shelf. "He says a person can rise against their circumstances and difficulties to embrace whatever life throws at them."

"It's a lovely theory," Emmy said.

"Yes," he agreed. "Unlike Kant, who claims reason must be accepted as a priority."

He handed Emmy the book and returned to the kitchen. Then, he poured the hot carrot broth into the mugs on the table. The drink was becoming a popular substitute for coffee, but although it smelled nice, Emmy found it far less satisfactory.

"Thank you," she said, grateful for the gifts presented by the odd but thoughtful man. She appreciated how emotional he was and also how he always seemed to stay motivated.

"Emmy," he said as he took a seat beside her. "I think we should go to Zurich."

"Switzerland?" she asked. "Why? Are we not safe here in Berlin?"

"No, it's not that," he replied. "Well, not exactly. Look, there's no work for you here, and I always had the intention to educate myself abroad. This war and this demand for patriotism is only contradicting my convictions."

"The theaters will open again, won't they?" she asked.

"Who's to say? Look at Russia. Before the war, they had a brilliant theater, and Germany was not far behind. But the current state of the world only indicates that everything genuine and sincere in either country is being crushed by external restraint."

Emmy knew he was right. Just a couple of years ago, the entertainment industry was thriving. Now, the cabarets and nightclubs across Europe were all closing. Even the Moulin Rouge in Paris had gone up in flames. The news reported that people in Montmartre thought they were being attacked by a German Zeppelin when they woke to alarms and loud sirens, but the fire was actually caused by an electrical malfunction. The auditorium and ballroom had been destroyed within minutes. Only the stage, protected by a heavy, fire-proof curtain, survived. Repairs to the building were unfeasible during the war, the news reported. No one knew if and when it would reopen.

"The importance of the theater is always inversely proportional to the importance of social morality and civil freedom," Hugo said, continuing his proposal. "Without freedom, there can be no performance."

Emmy thought about it. For herself, too, the theater was becoming just a memory. The cabarets that once lined the streets in bursts of color had all but been abandoned. It seemed the Belle Époque was over and with it, an era of optimism, peace, and prosperity. Entertainment was now replaced by explosions.

"I don't know," Emmy said, a bit uncertain. "Are you sure?" When it came to reason, Emmy typically sided with Nietzsche, though she mostly based her decisions on her own desires and passions. Switzerland wasn't a bad option, she considered. The war had been raging for more than a year, and unlike Belgium, the Swiss had managed to maintain their neutrality while remaining armed. To travel there, though, without any papers or money wasn't possible. Was it? What would they do once they got there? And when it came to Hugo, this man who showered her with affection, she still wasn't sure if she loved him.

"How will we get there?" she asked.

"We'll be like two tightrope walkers in the dark," he said. He told her about the blockades at the borders but how Switzerland was becoming a haven for foreign refugees and intellectuals. He said he knew some people there already: his friend Hans Richter and Ludwig Rubiner, an expressionist poet, and according to rumor, Vladimir Lenin, a revolutionary thinker from Russia.

Hugo reached out to Emmy across the table. His fingers warmed her cheek. "Come with me?"

Emmy thought about what she would have to leave behind. Not only her life in Germany but also her child. "What about Annemarie?" Emmy asked. "I can't leave her here in Germany."

"Your daughter will be safe with your mother in the countryside," Hugo replied confidently. "And if there is ever any doubt, I will rescue her myself."

Emmy thought for a moment about being a mother; then she remembered a play she performed a few years ago, called "The Wind," about the end of the world. In the play, a comet was expected to hit the earth, and everyone only had a few weeks left to live. She played the role of a funny little maid who did not believe the prophecy and eagerly took advantage of life's final weeks.

There were many times in Emmy's past when she thought the world might end, but she always believed there was nothing she could do except do what made her happy.

If she had never taken risks, she considered, she would still be back where she was from. Trapped under the isolated bell jar of the little port town. If she never would have left, she wouldn't have seen the world or loved so vastly or sang. She wouldn't have had any of the adventures that she had already had.

She looked at Hugo, who was waiting for her answer.

In his mind, it seemed, the future was still bright. Maybe, Emmy thought, Switzerland was the refuge for those who, like them, had kept the dream of freedom in their head.

She longed for new adventures and the uncertainties that came with it. Without such possibilities, she could not imagine being. Besides, alongside faith and love, hope was all they had. Together, they formed the highest and noblest values in all of human history. And just maybe, Hugo was the risk she needed to take for her own freedom.

ACT II

Zurich, Switzerland
Spring 1915 – Winter 1915

19

Moving to Zurich

Brum, brum brum, brum, brum, brum, brum, brum, ba-umf.

The rumbling of the train mocked Emmy's empty stomach, waking her before the deafening screech of the brakes.

"Hauptbahnhof Zurich, end station!" the conductor shouted into the cabin of the train.

Emmy gathered her belongings as she watched the other passengers stand. Hugo had hardly said a word since the journey began. He just sat across from her, looking out the window. She wished he would talk to her or at least tell her his plan. For an intellectual, he sure did make her feel a great sense of responsibility.

They hadn't brought much with them, a couple of suitcases with clothes, Hugo's typewriter, some books and what little money they had. They didn't know what they could expect from the journey, but Emmy had learned not to expect anything when traveling.

She had been to Bern, the capital of Switzerland, but not to Zurich, which was bigger and closer to the German border. Neither of them knew what to expect when they got there. The border patrols were inconsistent, and there were different systems in each region. Lucky for them, the small country hadn't yet introduced passport controls at all crossings, although there were whispers on the train that they would be in place by autumn.

It wasn't even summer, though, and even though the air was still cold, the sun outside was bright. The light-flooded through the open arches of the station's iron trestles, illuminating the path for the trains and the travelers.

Emmy looked around at all the well-dressed people. Everything looked beautiful, and everyone seemed happy.

On Bahnhofstrasse, a street famous for its shopping, women in long, flowing dresses and jaunty hats strolled alongside the shops and bank buildings. The men held walking sticks and wore things that made them look dapper, like monocles and double-breasted vests over ties. The buildings were built of solid stone and featured intricate decorations over the entrances. It reminded her a little of Paris, she thought, with its cosmopolitan feel.

On the square in front of the station, there was a great big fountain flowing with crystal-clear water. Blossoming linden trees lined the sidewalk, and the shops had two-story windows displaying expensive things to buy. Most pleasing to Emmy, though, was the city's energy. There was still a *joie de vivre*, which had been lost in Germany.

"Do you want to wait here?" Hugo asked. They were standing in front of a café in which small tables were lined up behind an oversized window pane. The guests sat with their drinks, looking out onto the street and watching the passers-by. Emmy stole a glance at the women sitting next to their friends, gossiping about life and enjoying the day.

"Relax," Hugo suggested. "I'll organize our accommodations."

"Are you sure?" Emmy asked. She wasn't sure she should let him go alone, but before she could suggest otherwise, he led her to a table and ordered her a coffee.

"I'll be back soon," Hugo said, kissing her forehead. Then, he crossed the street and boarded an electric tram.

"*En Guete*," the waiter said as he set down a steaming cup of coffee, sugar cubes and a silver bowl with bread.

"Oh," Emmy said nervously. "I don't believe we ordered this."

"The bread is on the house," he said. "Complementary."

Emmy looked at the offering, then back at the man. She wondered if he was serious. If he had even contemplated its value. Fresh bread was rare back home in Germany. Soft, golden pillows of dough. Surely, she thought, such a great treasure should be in a museum.

Emmy observed the other diners around her to see if they were also in wonder, but instead, she saw in bewilderment a man beside her mindlessly consumed his. His eyes focused on the newspaper, one hand holding a roll, the other piling on a forkful of steak tartare.

"Thank you," she said. "That's very kind." Suddenly, Emmy felt a little emotional. The waiter looked at her strangely, then let her be.

After a few minutes, the man next to her stopped eating. "Excuse me, miss?" he said, putting down his bread and fork. "Are you okay? You're crying."

"Me?" Emmy asked, assessing her emotions. She gasped for air and rubbed her hand under her nose. Why was she crying? What should she say? She wanted to tell the man about how bread did not exist back in Germany, but she didn't know how she should explain it. Should she mention that Germany's golden wheat fields had turned into blood-splatted battlefields, and she was just taken aback to see bread so fresh and abundant? She considered it, then thought it better not to say out loud where she had come from.

"I'm okay," Emmy said, thinking if she could blame her tears on the sun in her eyes. "The bread is just so good. There's just something very special about it. Perhaps, though, I only think so because it's so early in the morning…"

The man looked at her, waiting for her to continue, but Emmy didn't know what else to say.

"Okay, then," he said, seemingly satisfied with her response. "*En Guete*. Enjoy."

"Thank you," Emmy replied. She held up the bread and took a bite of it. "Yes," she said. "The bread is good. May we all be blessed to have it daily."

Emmy saved half the roll for Hugo, along with a few sips of coffee, which had turned cold by the time he got there, but he enjoyed it gratefully.

"I have some good news," he said, placing the empty cup down on the table. "I've found a room for us across the river, in the entertainment district.

20

First days in Zurich

Those first days in Zurich were like living in a dream. Each morning that Emmy woke up, she felt like life was worth living. As soon as the sun rose, she would get out of bed, then pull open the curtains and let the sunshine shine in.

"Come on, Dada," Emmy said, pulling on Hugo's feet. "Wake up. Let's go for a walk."

Hugo had been busy meeting friends and acquaintances practically every night since they had arrived in Zurich. The night before, he'd been out until 2 a.m. with Ludwig Rubiner, who was a poet and friend of Erich and Wedekind.

Emmy looked out the window to the cobblestone courtyard below. Their room, in the Hotel Weisse

Kreuz, was located in Niederdorf, in the old part of the city. The neighborhood was full of centuries-old, narrow, towering houses, their gables almost touching, and the streets were lined with small shops, restaurants and cafés, some painted in pale colors of spring.

The bed creaked as Hugo sat up, then groaned and yawned and put on a white t-shirt. Emmy gave him some time to get ready, then led him outside toward the Limmat River.

"Look!" Emmy said when they reached the water. There were swans floating by and seagulls soaring overhead.

"I know!" Hugo looked around in amazement. "Can you believe they're not stuffed?"

Emmy also stood there with wide eyes. None of it seemed real to her. The city was beautiful. It radiated elegance and intellect. The people seemed at peace on their Sunday stroll, walking leisurely along the river.

"Everyone is so relaxed here," she said.

"Well, maybe not everyone," Hugo said. "But they don't seem as compulsive as those in Germany, who confuse business cycles with life and their interests with fate. Yesterday, Rubiner said there's a growing movement. It seems he's becoming quite the central figure among those who fled to Switzerland. He and his wife also left Germany to escape the war. He spoke of many people I should meet, including some French and Russians."

"Oh?" Emmy asked without a hint of concern. She wasn't sure Hugo should get so well-connected, considering they were technically in the city illegally.

"Yes," he replied. "I think it's very likely we'll become friends."

Emmy smiled to protect Hugo's ego. Even though she wasn't sure she agreed with his meetings, it was nice, at least, to see him enthusiastic. "That's good," she said. She, too, believed the war and violence were unjust, but she didn't necessarily feel like sitting around all night and discussing it was a good way to spend her life.

Suddenly, the clock bells began to ring, joyful chimes that filled the city. The pitch was high, but the sounds came out slowly. It reminded her of a quote by a German philosopher, Jakob Böhem: "He to whom time is as eternity, and eternity as time, he is freed from all strife." She took a deep breath and promised to never waste away even a second.

"I think I can feel at home here," Hugo said, squeezing Emmy's hand. It felt strong and protective over hers.

Emmy smiled at the idea. It was true, she considered. Although they weren't Swiss, it was quite easy to feel like they belonged. There was something unique about the city that felt welcoming and accepting. Already since they had begun their walk, Emmy had heard people speaking multiple languages: Russian, French, Romanian, English and Italian. Even

High German dialects like her and Hugo's were common.

She and Hugo explored the city until the sun began to set, taking in the fresh air and new sights and sounds. They ate an apple at a farmer's market, which was set up on a bridge, and drank water from public fountains, which flowed fresh and freely. They sat at the lake, watching the boats gliding to and from the center of the city. Then, they made their way back up Bahnhofstrasse toward the main train station where they had first arrived.

It was Sunday, so the shops were closed, but their windows were illuminated by electric lamps. One store, in particular, caught Emmy's eye. She looked up, standing in the grandeur of the glass-covered building.

Hugo squeezed Emmy's hand as a signal to get going. He didn't appreciate anything materialistic or expensive. It had been a while, though, since Emmy had bought anything nice for herself, and the mannequins looked so exotic, clothed in luxurious fashions.

"Okay," Emmy said with slight disappointment. They couldn't afford any of the nice things anyway.

As they turned to cross back over the river, Emmy wondered when Hugo would address their state of affairs. They were still living off the pennies from the bottom of their pockets. Suddenly, a bright red light caught Emmy's eye. She looked up and read the sign.

"The Cabaret Bonbonniere," she said out loud. She squeezed Hugo's hand. "Let's go inside?"

21

Cabaret Bonbonniere

The walls of the Cabaret Bonbonniere were draped in red suede, and purple pagoda lights hung from the ceiling. There was a musician on stage playing the violin, and the waiters and staff looked smart and sophisticated.

Hugo and Emmy stood in the back, their eyes watching the stage. The ensemble was diverse, Emmy noted, both in acts and people.

"Maybe I should audition?" Emmy whispered as she looked around the theater. She looked up at Hugo for encouragement, but he just stood there quietly, watching the performance.

She knew how Hugo felt these days about the theater. He had practically denounced it just before their move to Zurich. If she remembered exactly, he had told her it made him feel the same as a, "man who had been suddenly decapitated."

Emmy had found his denunciation a little dramatic, even though he had proceeded to tell her about how the police were closing more and more theaters in Germany. The art was over, he had told her. It was "outrageous" that one could see a play these days, let alone perform in one.

Emmy, though, didn't need Hugo's approval. She would do what she desired like she always did. Knowing the answer deep down already, she grew tall with confidence and excitement.

***

The next day, Emmy walked back to the Cabaret Bonbonniere without Hugo, hoping to talk to the management before the show.

She didn't have an invitation, but she wasn't worried. She knew from experience that there were often dress rehearsals, and she would try to find the owner then. She was pretty good at selling herself, a skill she had learned from one of her previous jobs in her youth, in which she went door-to-door selling household supplies. She could convince many people of what they needed: ozone tablets, shoelaces, perfumed room fragrance. One scent, called "Blooming Meadows," had been her best seller. She could convince both housewives and butchers they needed one for each room.

Emmy pulled open the door to the café-cabaret and looked around. Then she walked to the front of the stage, where a group of men were standing.

"Come again to the left, but please, take slightly easier steps this time," one said.

"…and try to be a little more joyful," another added.

It had been more than a year since Emmy last performed. She tried to think back to her days at the Simplicissimus. The long curtains, the stage, the applause and attention.

"You're facing a turning point in your life! Act like it!"

Emmy was taken aback. "Excuse me?" she asked, but when she looked over at the man, she realized he wasn't talking to her.

"Excuse me?" the man repeated, this time looking directly at her.

"Oh," she replied, suddenly less secure. "Excuse me. I don't mean to interrupt. I'm also a performer, you see, and if you're looking for talent, I believe I could help."

The man looked at her critically, his eyes moving slowly up and down, which gave her just enough time to channel her charm.

"Okay," he said. "Let's see what you've got."

Emmy smiled politely and then handed him her coat, then walked onto the stage and began to sing. She had just gotten to the chorus when the man yelled out, "Stop!"

She wasn't sure why. She knew she had hit all the right notes.

"Your voice," the man in the middle said. "It's unusual. High, yet mature. Beautiful. You're not working someplace else?"

Emmy shook her head and smiled. She didn't even get to finish the song before the men agreed to hire her.

***

That night, and for many nights thereafter, Emmy was back on stage singing and performing. She wore elegant dresses, which the theater provided, and she transformed overnight from a demolished housekeeper to an elegant lady.

Between dancers and, painters and pianists playing Beethoven, Emmy sang, performed or read one of her poems.

Newspaper reviews called her couplets "evocative," and while it could have been taken with discouragement, Emmy took it as a compliment. She thrived in the theater life and grew braver with the praise, knowing that, at least for the time being, her talents would help dictate her way.

22

Warnings

That August, for the first time during the war, the Germans deployed flamethrowers in an attempt to clear out British trenches. At three in the morning, the grounds became alight in fire, and by sunrise, a total of 2,000 men had died.

Meanwhile, in Russia, the Germans had captured Warsaw, which seemed to give them a sense of invincible strength because, subsequently, they unlawfully torpedoed a British passenger liner off the coast of Ireland. Two American passengers were killed in the event, which alarmed U.S. President Woodrow Wilson. Now, according to *The Washington Post,* the United States was considering sending a million troops overseas.

Hugo told Emmy about the news with urgency in his voice, but the war seemed further away for her now. They were in Switzerland, a landlocked island surviving on its own. Besides, it was summer, and she was making good money from Cabaret Bonbonniere's sophisticated clientele.

***

Emmy was getting ready to go on stage when she saw two men in suits enter the building. At first, she didn't think much of it but then overheard them using formal pronouns.

She watched for a few minutes as the two men stood beside the owner, then looked around the room at the other performers. No one else seemed to be bothered by their presence, but Emmy felt uncomfortable by the seriousness they exerted.

She watched the men cautiously from behind the curtain. Then she saw the owner reach for his wallet. The men looked at his card then, handed it back to him, then walked over to the bar and started talking to the waiters.

Emmy turned around, wondering if anyone else had seen what was happening. They kept asking everyone for their identification.

"Go on for me," Emmy said to another performer standing behind her.

"What?" the woman asked, looking back at Emmy.

"I don't feel well," she said, hurrying out the back door.

Emmy stood, shaking, next to the garbage bins. Her heels balanced atop piles of soggy leaves and cigarette butts. It wasn't yet dark, but the sun had already set. If someone was looking for her, she thought, it wouldn't be difficult.

She tried to calm down and shallow her breath, but her mind only focused on the times she had previously been arrested. How easy it had been for men to accuse her of guilt, even when they didn't know what she did or didn't do.

She looked around the corner, trying to decide if she should move. It would be less suspicious, she thought if she stood outside the entrance. She squeezed past the garbage bins and slipped around the corner.

"Emmy?"

Emmy froze. Her heartbeat was heavy in her chest, but her breath held still.

"Aren't you supposed to be on stage?"

She turned around and saw the owner, who was lighting a cigarette in his mouth.

"I was, um…" she tried not to be suspicious. "I was just out here getting some fresh air. I'm not feeling well."

"They didn't find you then?"

"Who?"

"The *authorities*," he said in a sarcastic tone. "They were checking everyone's papers. They had reports of actors who had been sent from Germany to perform covert propaganda."

"What? That's ridiculous," she said, even though she could believe it. Hugo and Erich had both warned her about the government's involvement in theater. But from what she knew, the accusations of propaganda were drawn from fear and not experience. She herself still avoided patriotic songs, and all the acts she had seen at the Cabaret Bonbonniere had never mentioned politics.

"I know you're not Swiss," the owner said with a hint of regret in his voice. "Even though you look like one and can sing without an accent."

"Thanks for the compliment," she replied, somewhat under her breath. "I prefer not to identify with a specific country, but I was born in the north of Germany. My mother is Danish."

"Do you have any papers?"

"Not with me," she said. "I'm in the process of applying, but the last time I tried, I was accused of forging a false passport. I don't know why it's necessary, really, to have such documentation. I've already traveled and sung all across Europe without identification. And my father, he was German, but he navigated around the world twice without seeing a border.

The man looked back at Emmy softly when she mentioned her father. His gray, bushy eyebrows lowered on his friendly brown eyes.

"I'm sorry," he said, as he tossed his cigarette on the floor. "You can't play here anymore. I can't be responsible for the consequences of hiring undeclared foreigners."

***

When Emmy got home, she fell onto the bed crying. She and Hugo had just moved out of the hotel and into a room of their own. It had been difficult to find something they could afford, but a friend of Hugo's knew the owner who rented them the room. It was in a dark alley and for minimal rent, which the landlady had generously offered after mistaking Hugo for a famous painter.

"It's okay," Hugo said, sitting next to her. "Something else will come along. We've gotten by so far."

As he consoled her, Emmy tried to think of why she was really upset. Whether it was the lack of foreseeable income, or the simple fact she was rejected. She had been in Zurich for nearly three months, and while life was better than in Germany, they were hardly well-off.

She and Hugo never talked about money. It was far more important for them to stay wealthy in hope and courage. She knew, though, that the luxuries of Switzerland came with high expenses. And now, there was no chance that she could work.

Emmy turned her head away from Hugo and dug her face deeper into the pillow.

"I met with Fritz Brupbacher today," Hugo said, placing his hand on her back. "After his lecture at the Weissen Schwan, I went up and introduced myself. His teachings are profound, and you should hear his language skills. He switches between *Züritüïtsch* and Russian so quickly."

Emmy didn't care who Fritz Brupbacher was, although she was jealous that he could speak in the local Zurich dialect. Maybe if she could speak Swiss German, the theaters would allow her to sing again. She rolled over on the bed and looked up at Hugo, who hadn't stopped talking.

"He spoke about Russia's peasant, pre-economic lifestyle and how it is in direct contrast to the Americanized West. Most of the audience rejected his ideas, but as a leftist revolutionary, I think he understood that people here just love material goods."

Emmy was all too aware of Hugo's disinterest in consumerism. He rarely purchased anything he didn't really need. He went on and on about how a "revolt in materialistic philosophy was more necessary than a revolt of the masses," but Emmy just thought it was his way to find comfort in not having any money.

"He asked what I was doing in Zurich, and I told him about our situation," Hugo said. "Brupbacher was born here in the city, and he said he knows some of the local merchants. He said Franz Jelmoli, the man who owns the big glass department store, might be hiring. He said he could introduce us for an interview."

Emmy remembered the glass palace and the gowns that glittered in the window. But while she was optimistic about the job, her true fears were deeper than money. If she wasn't allowed to sing, she considered, she would rather not live.

She turned back around to bury her face again in the pillow.

"Everything will be okay," Hugo said. "Don't worry."

Despite not fully believing him, she found Hugo's confidence comforting. She knew there was no point in worrying about what could come tomorrow, but it was getting harder to believe that life would go back to normal.

As the church bells chimed outside their window, Emmy counted the hours to twelve, then rolled over and closed her eyes as Hugo sat next to her, rubbing her back.

***

The next morning, Hugo and Emmy walked to Jelmoli's department store. They crossed the river where the swans swam beside them, walked up the cobblestoned streets lined with boutique shops and old apartment buildings, and toward the main shopping street where the glass-covered palace was.

Emmy was nervous, suddenly worried she hadn't worn the right dress. But Hugo marched right in, free of the fear of judgment. Inside, a woman selling perfume stopped them and asked if they would like a sample, but Hugo interrupted her and said they were looking for Mr. Jelmoli. She looked a bit surprised but agreed to show them to customer services, who took down their names before leading them to the owner's office.

Emmy stood in the doorway. It was well-lit, with a large chandelier hanging from the ceiling. A few people were working in the back, standing over a table piled with vividly colored fabrics. In the center of the room, an elderly man stood over a large mahogany desk. Their guide went over and whispered something to him, then motioned to Emmy and Hugo to sit down.

"So," the man said, taking a seat at the table across from them. "Brupbacher sent you."

The man was well over 50, Emmy guessed. He had suntanned skin, a handsome, wrinkled face and sported a cheeky, well-groomed mustache. She found he fit the role quite nicely: an impresario who ruled over beautiful things.

"Yes," Hugo said. "My name is Hugo Ball, and this is my wife Emmy."

Emmy looked at him, surprised.

"We're both very hardworking, and we would be great with your customers," he said.

Wife? Emmy repeated the word in her head.

"I see," the impresario said after a moment. "Unfortunately, with the state of things, I worry we already have more staff than customers…"

It wasn't a great start.

"Do you speak Swiss German? Or French?" Jemoli asked, as if he would reconsider.

Hugo looked at Emmy, giving her a chance to speak.

"I speak French," Emmy said, suddenly gaining her confidence. "I lived and performed for a while in Paris." She wasn't telling the truth completely. She had actually just been on vacation there and spent weeks in the hospital, but she did perform in Belgium, where French was spoken, and she knew enough French songs to get by in conversation.

"Where are you from?" Jelmoli asked, looking at her curiously. "You speak such lovely, unusual German."

"Oh…" Emmy began. She cursed herself again for not knowing the Swiss dialect.

"My wife, the poor, pale thing, grew up in Leipzig, in the middle-eastern part of Germany," Mr. Jelmoli continued before she could answer his question. "Your accent is similar, but you look more…"

"Mr. Jelmoli," Hugo interrupted in an attempt to protect her and redirect the story. "Sir. You must have something you need help with at your impressive store. We're very trustworthy and versatile employees."

"No," Mr. Jelmoli said, shaking his head. He stood up from his desk. "I'm afraid at the moment, I can't think of anything except a few chores. But such things would be too simple-minded for you. Fritz said you were intellectuals. What is your real job, anyway?"

"Well," Hugo said, "I'm a writer. But before that, I worked as a theater director at the Kammerspiele in Munich."

Hugo looked at Emmy. "And my wife," he continued, again using the formality. "She's a poet and a singer. She sells out nearly every show, from the Cabaret Bonbonniere here in Zurich to the Simplicisimus in Munich."

"The Simplicisimus?" A young woman who had been sorting through the fabrics suddenly spoke from the back with delight. Mr. Jelmoli looked over at the young woman and then started to explain.

"Well, that's just dandy," he said. "My daughter and I are enthusiastic about theater. What kind of pieces did you perform in Munich?"

"You don't say!" Hugo answered happily. "Well, most recently, I produced plays by Frank Wedekind."

"Wedekind! That's why you look familiar," the young woman walked over to the desk where they were sitting. Emmy looked at her dress, which was long and formal but cut low around her collar and cinched at the waist. It had an exotic print that Emmy hadn't seen before, and over it, she was wearing a Japanese kimono.

"You know Wedekind?" Emmy asked, smiling at the woman. Maybe she would be their ticket in. "We're quite good friends with him."

"Oh, I just love him," the young woman said, growing more excited. "I met him once, personally, at a party at his castle that he threw for my best friend…"

"Yes," Hugo replied, not so much interested in the woman's story. "Emmy sings many of the songs that he's written."

"Well, that's great!" Mr. Jelmoli exclaimed. "You can let us know when he puts on his next show." The old man smiled affectionately at his daughter. "My daughter and I would be happy to support you."

Emmy looked at Hugo, waiting to see how he would reply.

"Of course," Hugo said, taking a deep breath. If he was disappointed, Emmy thought, he didn't show it. "Thank you very much for your time and your offer."

"Good luck with the job search," Jelmoli said before showing them to the door. "Until we meet another time."

Another time, Emmy thought, repeating his words in her head. So often, those words had been enough to keep her from being discouraged, yet somehow as he said it, they felt the most futile.

23

Anarchy

Emmy's first impression of Switzerland soon lost its luster. The longer she stayed in Zurich, the more she felt like a foreigner. One didn't have to listen carefully to understand the sense of superiority that began to spread across the neutral country. Even the politest Swiss could be heard calling Zurich "little Berlin."

News on the Western Front had been relatively quiet, but the Germans, French, and British were still actively fighting. Just across the borders, the neighbors were battling, attempting to infiltrate each other's cities and railways. The British tried to push the Germans out of France by deploying plumes of Chlorine gas onto the fields. The newspapers published a photo of soldiers walking through the poisonous clouds. Germany was named the victor of the Battle of Loos, but Emmy wasn't sure how anyone could claim success for killing 8,000 of 10,000 men in four hours.

***

Emmy looked at the view over the city of Zurich. She was sitting next to Hugo on the stone wall that was once a fort that protected the city. Suddenly, she wondered what life must be like back home and how her daughter, Annemarie, was doing.

"What do you think it's like in Germany now?" She turned to look at Hugo.

"I'm sure it's no fairytale," Hugo said. "Not as it once was, anyway."

"Yes," Emmy said sadly. She allowed herself a moment to remember her childhood. The small, unpaved roads of the port town by the sea, the corner store, filled with vases of raspberry candies and sugar sticks to chew on. She wondered if Annemarie had tried the candy. If she was playing with the other kids in the neighborhood, skipping stones and singing.

Hugo put his arm around Emmy's shoulders, then pulled her in closer to his body. "You know," he said. "Once upon a time, in the heart of Europe, there was a land that seemed to have a perfect breeding ground ready for an unselfish ideology. Germany will never be forgiven for ending this dream."

Emmy looked over at Hugo and placed her hand on his lap. "Hugo, do you remember when we first arrived, and you said you felt like you could be a real Swiss?"

"Yes," he replied, kissing her cheek. "I still think I could. I'm more than eager to give up my Germanity."

"Hugo," Emmy said, looking around to ensure no one overheard him. "We will never be Swiss, and we won't ever have the accents or papers to prove it. We can't get jobs… I can't sing. What are we doing here? We can't make a living."

Hugo didn't say anything at first. He just hung his head down while she looked straight ahead of her. A big church across the river was glowing in the sunset. The street in front of it led to the alley where they were living. Everything looked perfect, but Emmy knew it was just the perception.

"I overheard a woman outside the bakery today saying that a tailor, a cobbler and a copper-maker have all been arrested in our neighborhood," Emmy said. "Did you know that?"

"Yes," Hugo replied. "I've also heard of these anarchist investigations, but so far, they have only led to mystification."

"Maybe," Emmy responded. "But it seems more people are being sought out and deported."

"It is a sad thing when one's harmless daily routines can take on such a dangerous significance," Hugo said. "We're all surrounded by terrible secrets. By this, *bloody aura*." He emphasized the last words. "Even the

Swiss are starting to doubt their own neutrality. I'm sure that's why I can't find a publisher."

Emmy couldn't believe he was complaining about not getting published. She couldn't sing!

"I'm worried Brupbacher's paper is going to be the next to be censored," he said. "The Swiss are starting to ban all printing of political opinions. They're worried the world is doubting their neutrality. They're threatening a 5,000 Franc fine and six months of jail for anyone who denigrates a foreign person in spoken word or image."

Emmy took her hand off Hugo's lap and turned to face him.

"Censorship only limits the diversity of opinions," Hugo said poignantly. "What we should be doing is sharing our thoughts. We should be celebrating and publishing international authors. Kandinsky, Marinetti, Apollinaire. Writers whose aim it is to regenerate society through artistic mediums, not forces. Unfortunately…" he waved his hand dismissively over the city, "there seems to be little interest for diverse opinions in Zurich."

Emmy shook her head. What good were stories if she couldn't tell hers.

"Are you hungry?" Hugo asked. The sky was getting dark.

Emmy nodded.

"Come," he said. "I know somewhere we can get a hot meal for cheap."

***

Emmy hadn't expected to dine at the Russian community center, but she couldn't be upset. The peaches, soup and bread looked delicious, and it only cost a few cents. It was loud in the restaurant, but she also found it charming. The diners sat at long wooden tables, and the mood was relatively joyful.

She followed Hugo, carrying her tray of food through the canteen.

"*En Guete*," Hugo said as he passed by a table of men. "Enjoy your meal," he said to another. "Good evening, Sir," he continued. "Nice to see you."

Emmy didn't recognize any of the men and was slightly taken aback that Hugo was being so friendly with them.

"You just missed Lenin," a man told Hugo as they sat down at a table. "He's on his way to a conference in Zimmerwald."

"Ah," Hugo said with some disappointment. "That's a shame. I would have liked to hear his opinion on things."

Emmy wasn't sure what Hugo was talking about. She paid little attention to socialist gossip, but she had heard the name Vladimir Lenin before, which sparked her attention. Hugo had said he was a Russian revolutionist who was living in exile in Switzerland. A few years ago, the man had made international news when his 21-year-old brother was executed for attempting to assassinate the Russian Emperor. Lenin, who was probably now in his mid-40s, was rumored to be encouraging others to overthrow the government.

The men at the table spoke in a heavy dialect, so Emmy wasn't able to catch everything they said next, but it was something about Germany and Russia and Zurich's Social Democratic party.

The Swiss may have been censoring the press, but it seemed as though no one at the Russian dining hall was worried about sharing their opinion. Maybe, Emmy considered, it was because the Russians were fighting a different war, further from the Swiss borders.

"All parties should be defeated," a man beside her declared with a mouthful of bread. "This should be an international war. An armed uprising of peasants against the bourgeoisie. Only then could an actual revolution come."

"Here, here," another man agreed. "Total destruction could serve as a healing force. Once the materialistic society is destroyed, working-class intellectuals and economists can rise up to shape a new Europe."

Emmy watched as Hugo shook his head in dismissal.

"I don't know," Hugo said. "I'm no anarchist. I've examined myself carefully. I could never bid chaos welcome, throw bombs, blow up bridges, or do away with ideas."

Emmy was glad that he had said it. She remembered how Erich had been labeled an anarchist for the articles he had published as a student. He had still been practically a child when he was awarded the label, simply for writing an op-ed about his unpleasant teachers.

Emmy wondered how Erich was doing. If he was still in Berlin. If he was avoiding the war and staying out of trouble. As she took another spoonful of soup, she told herself to remember to write to him when they got home.

The conversation continued as they finished their meal, and in a kind of self-imposed exile, Emmy kept listening. What the men were saying made Emmy think even more about her past, but while she took in their theories, she also envisioned a future without the fears and uncertainties. It was better not knowing, she thought, when and where they might all be defeated.

24

Autumn

Over the next few weeks, Emmy waited for good news to come along while Hugo, in a way, grew even more distant. Practically every evening, he was out attending lectures with the students, even though he himself wasn't enrolled in the University.

When he would get home late in the evening, he would tell Emmy about his conversations and the people that he met. He told stories about men who had been exiled in Siberia and others so poor they smoked cigarettes rolled with newsprint.

Emmy, still without work and a little depressed, preferred to stay home and paint with watercolors or write instead of going out with him. Autumn had come, and so had the rain, and with everything going on outside, she found their apartment to be the most comforting place.

Hugo, even though he wasn't technically making any money either, did find work at a publication, where he shared an office with Fritz Brupbacher. Emmy still slightly resented the man for setting up the embarrassing meeting with Mr. Jelmoli, but Hugo said Brupbacher wanted to make it up to her by printing her poems in his paper.

Emmy did her best to pretend to forgive him and be the slightest bit interested in what Hugo would tell her. But he was always so serious when he told his stories. There was nothing beautiful or optimistic about the topic or prose. She could see nothing good that could come from it. She wished they could simply focus on their own future instead of worrying about what was happening in the world.

***

"They're planning an overthrow of the Tsar," Hugo said. "A revolution."

Hugo was sitting at the table where they worked and ate their meals while Emmy sat on the floor, sewing curtains from outdated fabric.

"What?" Emmy asked, looking up from her sewing. The word caught her attention. "Who is *they?*"

"The students," Hugo continued. "They have been meeting for years in Zurich, as well as Geneva and

Bern. It will be just like the French in the previous century. Oh, I hope and imagine a liberation for them."

Emmy didn't know much about the French Revolution, just which it was caused by discontent with the monarchy. The king had been executed by guillotine, along with his wife, Queen of France, Marie Antoinette.

"I don't know," Emmy said. "Must you be so involved in politics? I thought you didn't believe in anarchy."

"I don't," he said. "But the collapse is beginning to take on gigantic dimensions. Their entire civilization will ultimately be exposed as a sham."

"Why do you let it affect you so much, though, personally? Do you really believe you can help change the course of history?"

"I don't have any choice," Hugo said. "I cannot practice my ugly, political-rationalist studies without repeatedly immunizing myself. I have to engage in irrational things. If I like a political theory and its fantastic utopian poetry, I get stuck with my aesthetic circle until I can make sense of it. Maybe it's those of us who grew up in idyllic conditions, intimately connected with nature or religion, who are being severely seized by the state."

Emmy wondered if that last part was to enrage her, too, but unlike him, she was happier to keep her distance. Sure, she might agree with his views, but she didn't understand why he felt the need to be a voice for the cause.

"Think about it," he said. "This war will collapse Germany. Not just its old ideals but also as a breeding ground for all of civilization. We will be completely without any basis."

Bang! Bang! Bang!

Hugo and Emmy looked at each other. Someone was knocking at the door.

The first thought that ran through Emmy's head was that someone had overheard Hugo. There were spies, she remembered, people undercover who were arresting the bakers and tailors and cobblers.

"I'll get it," Hugo said, getting up from the table.

Emmy stood up from the floor and against the far wall in the kitchen, out of sight from the entry.

"Ah, good evening," Hugo said. Then, he began to speak in an informal, friendly tone. Emmy peaked her head around the corner to see who it was.

"Frau Sütterli," Hugo said. "What an unexpected surprise. I hope you're doing well?"

It was their landlord.

"Mr. Ball," the woman said, in a kind-of frail, old-lady voice. "These letters arrived in the post today. It's addressed to a Mr. Willibald. Do you know him?"

There was silence for a moment. "There must have been a mistake," Hugo said, laughing awkwardly. "I'll see to it that it's sorted."

Another moment of silence followed his reply, and though Emmy couldn't see their landlord's face, she could imagine her being disoriented.

"Oh, and Frau Sutterli, I'm glad you stopped by. It reminds me, I've been meaning to give you a painting." Hugo grabbed a framed print that was laying against the wall and handed it to her.

"Have a good evening," he said while urging her outside and gently closing the door.

Emmy walked slowly back into the center of the room. "How can you take advantage of that senile, old lady like that? What painting did you give her? My watercolor roses?"

She looked at Hugo, who opened the letters and then looked at her with fear.

"Emmy," he said, with an unusual sense of concern in his voice. "We have to leave the city. Tonight."

25

Geneva

Hugo and Emmy sat on the bank of Lake Geneva, staring melancholically into the water. The morning sky was foggy, and the water lacked any sparkle. It was only mid-August, but it felt like late fall. The last tender moments of summer had already gone.

They had been in Geneva for nearly two weeks. So far, they had gone undiscovered by police, but not being in prison didn't make things any easier. Emmy was still *sans-papiers,* meaning she couldn't get any work or lodging, and now, the police were looking for the man from Hugo's passport. They had hardly any money and relied only on the generosity of strangers. The whole situation verged on incoherence and absurdity.

Emmy looked over at Hugo, who was hanging his legs off the pier, watching fishermen cast lines for the fish. His shoes were tattered, just like the first pair she had seen him in. She didn't want to remind him, but she realized then they were poorer than the fish.

"So…" she said hesitantly. "What are we going to do now, Hugo?"

Hugo didn't say anything at first, then, after a while, he spoke up. "I don't know. I wrote to Brupbacher today, and I apologized for not saying goodbye."

"Okay…" Emmy replied. "How does that help?"

"I also asked if he could loan us 50 francs."

"Hugo…" Emmy said, her voice growing with concern. "Look at us. We're practically beggars. What are we doing? We can't ask for such money from someone we hardly know. And even if he did loan us a few francs, how does it solve the issue of our hidden identities?"

Emmy had been trying to be calm throughout the whole ordeal, but she was beginning to lose patience with him. They had been going in and out of cheap hotel rooms and random people's homes. Every night, staying somewhere new, friends-of-friends of the Russian students or other acquaintances, like Brupbacher.

"Maybe you should just turn yourself in," Emmy said, without realizing she said the words out loud.

Hugo looked at her with a sense of fear. "What do you mean?"

"It's not so bad," Emmy said. "I've been to prison before."

But as soon as Emmy said it, she remembered how terrible prison was. The blatant lack of sunlight. The cold, gray walls. She heard Erich's words in her head. "Arrests are more common now that we're at war."

"Maybe you can just explain to the police who you are," she said, trying to think of a more practical solution. "It's not like you've done anything wrong, really. Just tell them they've printed your name incorrectly and you didn't have time to change it… or tell them you've gone by Willibald since you were a child, and Hugo is a nickname people call you."

"No," Hugo said. "You're right. I should turn myself in. Look at me. Every citizen who is only half as brave can see I am inferior."

Emmy stayed quiet. She didn't want to upset him further. She was sad for him, but she was also sad for herself. Of course, she didn't want him to go to prison, but she wasn't sure how they could evade it at this point. With all the investigations going on, it was only a matter of time until the police would find them.

"I've thought about it too," she said. "We can't go back to Germany. They will check us at the border. And even though they're being more lenient with women, they'll question me for being with you."

"Don't worry," Hugo said. "I'll make sure nothing happens to you."

She wanted to believe him, but she wasn't sure she did.

***

Emmy didn't mention their state of affairs again until Hugo woke up with a nightmare, sweating and yelling.

"Hey," Emmy said, sitting up next to him and trying to hold him still. "Hey, hey. It's okay."

She tried to steady his shoulders, which were shaking in his blue-striped pajamas.

"No," Hugo said, not yet fully conscious. "If language really makes us kings of our nation, then without doubt it is we, the poets and thinkers, who are to blame for this blood bath and who have to atone for it."

"You're having a nightmare," she said, trying to wake him.

Emmy knew Hugo had been stressed about their circumstance, but she didn't realize it would result in him being haunted by night visions.

"Don't worry," she said. "Everything is going to be okay."

Hugo woke up and then fell into her chest. Tears from his cheek flowed down her neck, and she held him tight against her, her fingers in his hair.

Emmy felt sorry for Hugo. She knew she was putting a lot of pressure on him to make everything better, and he really was trying to find work and make connections. He was too intellectual, though, always overthinking, and for being the fifth of six children, he sometimes acted as if he were the only.

Emmy believed that guilt is often related to one's youth, and she recalled Hugo telling her how strict his parents had been growing up. His father dealt in shoes and other leather goods – which was ironic, Emmy thought, since Hugo's shoes were always in a desolate condition. He had encouraged Hugo to leave school at age 15 and start an apprenticeship with a leather dealer instead of continuing his studies. The led Hugo to have a nervous breakdown, just like Emmy would experience when her expressions were stifled. Hugo told her how he used to cry and cry until he couldn't move. His parents had called a doctor, but medication didn't help. Finally, he was given a cure when the doctor suggested he go back to school.

Then, at the age of 19, Hugo completed a three-year course in one year. He studied philosophy, literature and politics; he had told Emmy. And among his favorite writers were Bakunin, Erasmus and Nietzsche.

"Nietzsche," Emmy said, having a sudden realization.

"What?" Hugo asked.

"What doesn't kill you makes you stronger."

Hugo looked up at her.

"Nietzsche," she said. "Right? Wasn't that his philosophy? Self-overcoming? Overcoming one's self. Rising above your circumstances to embrace whatever life throws at you?"

Hugo looked up at her, his eyes growing wider. "Well, yes," he said. "I suppose... but he also died of depression..."

"Listen, Hugo," Emmy said, interrupting. "I know it's scary. I'm scared, too. I see the same nightmares as vividly as you."

"I don't know what to do," Hugo said with tears still in his eyes.

"Let's go home," she said, placing her hand on his back. "We will go back to Zurich and figure it out. We'll talk to the police and explain our circumstances. And if I have to, I'll sing for them."

The last part was a joke, but Hugo didn't laugh. Instead, he tucked his head against her chest, slowly nodding in agreement.

***

The next day, Emmy and Hugo woke up early, gathered their belongings and took the train to Zurich. On the way, they passed vineyards and mountains, and wide farmlands and small villages with medieval castles. Emmy looked out the window at all of the beauty and thought, just maybe, everything would work out.

The next morning, though, she would realize she was wrong. When, just before six a.m., police showed up at their home. Accompanied by two police dogs, the men banged on their door, demanding to see "Mr. Hugo Ball." Emmy cried and tried to explain, but despite her pleas, they pushed her aside. As she fell onto the floor in despair, they took Hugo away.

26

Emmy Alone

It was the sound of the rain that finally woke Emmy up. A heavy patter of water bouncing off the cobblestones and rooftops. She pulled a blanket close to her, then reached for the windowsill to lift herself up.

She had been in a daze lately, unsure of even what day it was. All she knew was that more leaves had fallen from the tree in the courtyard, and the sun had set again without Hugo's return.

She looked out onto the narrow alley, where the rain puddles reflected the glowing streetlights. She opened the window to get some fresh air. The straps of her nightgown fell off her bare, bony shoulder.

It had been at least five days since Hugo's arrest, Emmy considered. She tried to count back in her head from the last time she saw him. They had returned from Geneva by train just before midnight, and then, before dawn, they were woken up by police. She would rather not recount the scene. It was all so dramatic. There were police dogs barking, and she had been crying.

Emmy picked up a small glass bottle off the windowsill and took a sip. Five days, and she still hadn't stepped out of their apartment. After Hugo's arrest, their landlord, Frau Stutterli, came by and told Emmy she had until the end of the month to get out. Emmy remembered how the old lady glared at her in disgust and how she had simply thanked the woman and agreed to move. In all honesty, though, she didn't know what to do. With what little money she had, she could hardly afford stale bread.

Lost in a high of hunger and morphine, Emmy worried her only options to avoid destitution were dwindling down to petty crime and prostitution. She had nowhere else to go. She was a stranger on the streets of Zurich. Aside from the men who knew Hugo, she didn't know anyone.

Outside, the rain was calming, and Emmy watched as people from a tavern across the alley walked outside to smoke. The dusk sky lit their bodies in a spectral, ghost-like glow. The women's faces were painted and their hair was done up.

As Emmy considered joining them, a warm, calming feeling overtook her. She turned her face toward the moon and closed her eyes. "Love me free of all my sins," she whispered, then walked outside.

She wasn't proud of the things she sometimes had to do, but sometimes, there was no option but to do the things she had to. It wasn't as if she couldn't feel the horror, unable to free herself from being put on the table.

"Dear Miss, what do you cost?" a man asked, standing outside the cigar shop.

Emmy looked at the man. He had a beard but a soft face. She walked with him down the street then whispered in his ear.

***

At the beginning of the previous century, there had practically been a heyday of commercial love. But now, prostitution in most of Europe was seen as the decay of middle-class morality. Emmy, like most of her friends, dismissed the judgements as bourgeois double standards and reckless exploitation. Prostitution had been outlawed in Zurich for nearly 20 years, but if the police got involved, it was only the woman who got arrested.

Niederdorf, where she and Hugo had been living, was the entertainment district, which meant there were also brothels among the restaurants and theaters. The owners were mostly former performers themselves, who knew how to earn a living off entertaining gentlemen. Before the war began, promiscuity was practically taken for granted. Now though, most men didn't want to provide payment. They either complained they were too poor themselves or claimed like soldiers, they should get women for free.

***

After such an event, Emmy always felt a little emptier, even if she were a small amount wealthier.

She couldn't decide whether to try to find something to eat or go straight back home, so she just walked around the city, attempting to exist gracefully.

The city was quiet until the church clock struck midnight. A few people walked along the sidewalks, leaving from restaurants or closing shops. As Emmy reached Bellevue, the junction where the river meets the lake, she heard an old Austrian hymn being played on a piano, which reminded her of Hugo.

She stood for a moment in the middle of the crossing, trying to figure out what direction the music came from. Then, drawn to the song, she followed it down to a dimly lit bar.

She couldn't bring herself to go inside, even though she wanted to. So, she just stood outside the door, trying to recite the lyrics. She had sung it once, she remembered, at the Simplicissimus, the night she had met Hugo.

She stood against the brick façade of the building, then slid down to the ground. She could feel herself on the verge of another breakdown. Life had been so cruel lately, she thought in pity. She was tired of living in squalor and poverty. Still, she knew it wasn't only her who suffered.

***

"Extra, extra!"

Emmy woke up to a boy yelling about the news and holding the paper. She had fallen asleep in the street. The sun had risen. She started to panic.

"Germans Capture Russian Fortress in Gallipoli Campaign!" the boy shouted. Emmy watched as a man paid for a newspaper, then stood in the street reading.

Emmy stood up slowly, trying to be discreet, brushing off the dust from her coat and rubbing the sleep from her eyes. But then – she thought she might be just seeing things – she noticed a sketch on the back of the paper.

"Excuse me," she said to the man who was reading the paper. "Do you think you can spare the last page?"

The man looked at her like she was untouchable, then handed her the newspaper and walked away.

Emmy held the paper in front of her, the black and white print sending a clear message. Above the image, the title read, "Meet the artist, Reinhold Rudolf Junghanns – a painter of dancers and muses."

She hadn't thought about Rudi, but of course, he could help her. She would write to him. She slipped the newspaper under her coat and ran back to her apartment.

***

"Dear Junghanns!" She used his last name only to emphasize his fame.

"I beg you if it is possible for you to send me a few monies?" She didn't mean to ask for money right away, but she knew he would forgive her.

"I would be very grateful to you, Dear Junghanns," she continued, "if you might send a little money. Because I have nothing to eat right now."

Emmy debated going into detail about the tribulations of her life. Hugo's arrest, her lack of a passport, the morphine, but there wasn't any need to, she thought, so she didn't.

"Of course," she wrote, "If I can somehow repay you, I'll send it all back to you. You have my word."

Before she signed off, she wrote a note of congratulations, telling Rudi how happy she was to see him doing so well.

"My warmest congratulations," she said. Then signed her name below, "Please, don't forget your Emmy."

27

Happiness and Despair

It was in those last days between summer and fall when Emmy found herself worse than she had ever felt before. Her hair was in knots and hadn't been combed out in days. The glass bottle that she had relied on was now empty on the floor.

Hugo stood over her, looking down on her, as she lay face-up in bed. She blinked, not knowing if what she saw was real or a hallucination. "Good morning," he said. He leaned over and kissed her as if she was Sleeping Beauty.

"Hugo," Emmy said, trying to sit up.

Hugo smiled at her. He looked, well, great, actually. She blinked again and rubbed her eyes, still unsure if she was in a dream or reality.

"You're unwell," Hugo said. "I'm so sorry. It's all my fault. I promised you that you'd be safe and that we would have a better life here."

Emmy groaned and pulled the covers over her head. She didn't want to listen to his regrets as much as she didn't want him to see her so weak and reckless.

"I've taken care of everything," he said, pulling open the curtains. The sunlight poured in. "You don't have to worry anymore." He walked to the kitchen and turned on the faucet, then returned to her with a glass of water.

"Emmy," he said. "Look at you. I want to paint flowers on your hollow cheeks."

At least he didn't catch her passed out on the street, she considered.

"My little seahorse," he said, putting his hands on her face. "Everything is better now, you'll see. I came to Zurich to stay ahead of the game, and we will. Don't give up yet."

Emmy didn't know why he was so energetic. Did he not just come from prison?

"I'll be right back," Hugo said, kissing her forehead. "Drink some water and stay here and sleep."

Emmy watched as he gathered some papers, then blew out a burning candle on the table and left.

***

"Life is wonderful!" Hugo exclaimed upon his return.

Emmy looked at him suspiciously while he removed his coat. She had gotten out of bed, but she was still wearing her nightdress and her hair was still a mess.

"I found us a place to stay," he said. "Near the church."

"What?" Emmy asked, still confused by his return. Each time Emmy had gone to prison, she had become paralyzed with fear, but now, looking at Hugo, it seemed as if he had been on vacation.

"I talked to a friend who has an attic for rent," he said. "He said it's getting more crowded in Zurich because of the growing immigration. Living space is getting scarce, so I'm thankful."

"Hugo," Emmy said. "What's happening? Were you not just behind bars?"

"Oh, yes," he responded. "But it hasn't harmed me. The police weren't concerned about me avoiding German military service, but they know I'm not a painter from Hanover."

Emmy nodded slowly, trying to comprehend what he was saying without disturbing her headache. "So, now everything is fine with you?" she asked. "Meanwhile, I've been here, practically destitute. I've

173

been writing to friends in Germany to send money. We have nothing."

"We will be okay," he said. "I'll sell everything I own if I have to."

He didn't have much, Emmy wanted to tell him. She watched him as he looked around the room. She had already thought of what she could sell while she was sitting there by herself, starving. All they had were two travel bags, a few worn books and Hugo's suit.

"I did consider it..." she said, as she watched him hold his sight on his possessions. "It's not exactly useful at the moment, is it?"

Emmy saw he was disappointed with the idea but that he was beginning to understand the reality she'd been living while he was being cared for in prison. A formal suit was not worth holding onto when there were bigger issues.

"If you can't use your tailcoat, maybe you should sell it," she said, trying to say it in a way that wouldn't hurt his feelings. "That seems to be the most reasonable option. If it later turns out that you can't be without a tailcoat, then I'm sure you'll find the money again to buy one."

Hugo's smile faded.

"You're right," he said with a sigh. "If the tailcoat has been without me for so long, I can probably be without the tailcoat."

He picked up the box and looked inside. "Come," he said. "I'll show you our new home."

28

Treasures

Their new home on Kirchgasse was a sight to be seen. It was four minutes away and five stories tall. They had to climb fifty-eight narrow stairs to a small door at the top, which led to an attic that Hugo barely fit in.

The room itself was an open space, just below the rooftop beams. A few meters wide and not as quite deep, with a chimney running through the middle and an old mattress on the floor. Low on the wall was one great, big window, and when Emmy bent down to look out, she could see half of Zurich.

Hugo's optimism, which he had apparently regained in prison, slightly rubbed off on Emmy. In the following days, they ate well and stayed warm, sleeping together and dreaming of a better future.

Instead of selling his formal suit, Hugo had been wearing it, and left their home early each morning to try to find work as a bellboy or waiter. They were doing great, or at least that's what he told his mother when he wrote to her in his letters.

"Let her come," Emmy said. "Your mother would love Switzerland."

"That's ridiculous," Hugo replied. "She better not do something so stupid."

Hugo was sitting cross-legged in the bed, reading a letter from his sister that had arrived that afternoon. She claimed his mother didn't approve of his lifestyle in Switzerland and was threatening to come to Zurich to get him.

"I don't see why not," Emmy said.

"My mother doesn't understand, Emmy. She's a devout Catholic. She knows nothing of my private experiences; that I tend to compare my own being with that of the nation's."

"Well, honestly," Emmy said, "I don't understand that either."

"How can you not?" Hugo replied bitterly. "It's almost a matter of conscience to perceive a certain parallel."

"Why does it matter where one is from?" Emmy said defensively. "Does it not matter where you are now? A person is not given the option to decide where they are born."

"I don't expect you to understand," Hugo said, getting up off the bed. "You're just like the others."

"Well, please, Hugo," Emmy said, not sure who exactly he was comparing her to. "Explain it to me. Tell me why it's worth fighting more against a war than what we have in our kitchen."

Emmy looked around the room. "Oh wait! We don't even have a kitchen! Hugo, can't you see? We can't live like this forever."

"I'm trying! What do you want me to do?"

Emmy looked at him. His head almost hit the ceiling.

"You want me to sell the suit?" He asked, pulling it off the hanger on the backside of the door. "Fine, I'll sell the suit."

"You don't have to be so upset," Emmy replied defensively. "It's not about money."

"No," he said, bowing under the doorframe. "It is. You're right." He stepped out of the attic and slammed the door.

Emmy heard his steps echoing down the stairwell. She thought about calling after him but, instead, let the sound of his footsteps fade away. Then, when it was quiet, she crawled over to the window and looked out for him.

"It's just a coat!" she yelled down when he appeared. He didn't look up. He just threw his free hand into the air.

Emmy watched as he headed down the cobblestone lane toward the church towers. The long box with his tailcoat was tucked under his arm.

"Hugo! Wait," Emmy cried. Then she put on her shoes and ran after him.

It wasn't really about the money, Emmy considered as she ran down the five flights of stairs. But money did have a certain relationship to one's being, didn't it?

She followed the street toward the intersection by the lake, where the linden trees grew beside a café. The sun was setting, and the sky was full of pinks and purples. She tried to look for someone tall, with a big box under their arm, but after a few minutes of searching, she thought she had lost Hugo.

When she reached the river's mouth, she saw a crowd of people gathered on the sidewalk as if they were listening to a busker. As she got closer, though, she realized they were watching a group of officers who were standing around a big, white box.

At first, Emmy thought she should turn around to avoid the officers, but then, just like his mother, she had felt some kind of responsibility to care for Hugo.

"Excuse me," she said, making her way through the crowd.

"Hugo?" she spoke softly, approaching the officers from behind. They turned and looked back at her as if she was in their way.

"Do you know this man?" one of them asked.

"Yes, he's my husband," she replied, even though he wasn't. "Is everything okay, officers?"

"He was trying to climb the banister and jump into the lake."

She looked at Hugo, who was on the ground next to his box, visibly shaking.

"There must be a mistake," Emmy said, gently squeezing between the men to reach Hugo. "He wouldn't jump into the lake. He just likes to admire the fish."

The policemen looked at Emmy suspiciously as she tried to think of what else to say.

"We haven't been able to get a fishing license, you know, with the rations in place. But we do hope to get one soon. Hugo is very good at fishing, and the lake, it's so beautiful..."

Emmy was still talking when the officers seemed to get bored. They started mumbling something in the local dialect, then turned to walk away. When they were gone, and the crowd dispersed, Emmy helped Hugo stand up off the floor.

"I'm sorry," she said, wrapping her arm around his back. "I didn't mean to pressure you so much. You can keep the suit. We'll find another solution."

"No," he said. "I'm sorry, too. Sometimes, I fall into a slight madness."

"You weren't really going to jump into the lake, were you?"

"No…" he said. "I was just balancing the box on the ledge to tie my shoe, then it almost fell over, and well… the shortest way of self-help is to renounce one's work, anyway."

Emmy wasn't sure what he meant again.

"Come, Dada," she said, holding onto his hand. "Let's go for a walk. I'll carry your coat."

They took the long way home through the winding alleys. The restaurants were getting busy, and the shops were all closing. Every once in a while, Emmy would stop to admire a storefront, appreciating the beautiful things in the window.

"I'm sorry," she said, acknowledging they had just fought about money. "I can't help it. The displays are designed to catch your eye."

Emmy scanned through the items under the bright lights. An alarm clock, a pair of boots for hiking, a used typewriter.

"Good evening." A man was standing outside the shop's door, his arms crossed, addressing them.

"Good evening," Emmy replied sweetly.

"Are you interested in something?"

"Oh, no, that's okay," she said. "I see you've already closed your shop."

"If you'd like to buy something, you can take a look around," he said.

"No, thank you," Hugo said. "We're not buying anything."

"Well, we don't really know that yet," Emmy replied in embarrassment, giving Hugo a nudge. "I was just admiring the music box in the window."

"Ah, yes," the man replied. "I just got it in this morning." He went inside to retrieve it from the display, then showed her how to play the song by twisting a small key.

It was a lovely tune, Emmy thought. It had a delicate, high pitch, like a bird singing. "Oh!" she exclaimed. The music made her so happy. "It's lovely. How much does it cost?"

"For you?" The man looked her up and down. "Two francs-fifty."

Emmy thought about the offer. Her mother had always told her that asking about prices without buying anything was greedy.

"Or, since you're my prettiest client today, I can offer it on special offer for two francs."

Emmy knew she wasn't going to buy it. They couldn't afford it, even with the discount.

"I would like it very much," she said. "But you see, we're also currently in the market to sell. Might you be looking to buy a nice tailcoat?"

"What?" The man replied. He looked at the suit as Emmy opened the box. "No, no," he said. "I don't run a clothing store."

"No, but… you could," Emmy suggested. "Why not? You could give us a small down payment and then

181

sell the tailcoat for new. You would make a commission."

The man shook his head again. He was starting to look offended.

"It's no use," Hugo whispered to Emmy, pulling at her arm to leave.

"But what about the music box?" she replied. The storekeeper rolled his eyes and turned to go back inside his shop.

"Maybe," she suggested. "I could make a deposit of fifty cents now to reserve it? I will definitely pick it up tomorrow or next week if I'm in the area."

"I'm sorry," the man replied. "Full payments only."

Emmy bowed her head down sadly. "I understand."

Hugo kept hold of Emmy's hand as they left the store and walked toward their attic home. She was careful to hold her head low the whole time to not be pulled back in by sparkling windows. Money used to come easy to her, but now she couldn't even earn the bare minimum. She was sad that she no longer had the luxury to buy silks and small treasures.

It was Hugo who stopped them next, in front of a coiffure that had a display of shampoo in the window. Emmy looked at the handmade soaps and ornate glass bottles.

"DADA," Hugo said. "Hair-strengthening headwater."

Emmy tried to make sense of what Hugo was talking about, then she saw the poster hanging in the window. The words DADA was written above a beautiful young woman with long, curly hair that blanketed her body.

"You know," Hugo said. "The soldiers in the trenches wash their hair with cold tea."

"Oh, Hugo, do you have to be so bleak?"

They both looked at the advertisement, somehow under its spell. Typically, headwater was sold to men to prevent balding, but there was a woman in this ad, who smiled innocently, yet confidently. The longer Emmy looked at her hair, the more beautiful it became.

"This fat-containing hair water is available for three Swiss francs." Hugo read the advertisement out loud. "At *Parfumerie Bergmann & Co.*, and finer hairdressers in the city."

It was an insane amount of money, Emmy thought, but still, she decided she would buy it if she could. She herself had strong, dense hair, which she would like to be finer and softer.

"We spend 10 cents for soap," Hugo said. "Maximum."

"Yes, but ours smells like bad perfume and Lysol," she reputed. "Look, this one even promises happiness and luck."

Hugo laughed.

"So what?" he asked. "We should apply the soap because we're so miserable?"

Emmy sighed, he was right. However, she wondered if the soap could give her back the long, blonde curls from her youth.

They slowly turned away from the store and continued their walk through the old part of town while the sky grew darker and stranger characters came out. A mix of people between petty and bourgeois, and yet somehow, the two of them fit in perfectly.

While they walked, they talked about money, lost treasures and material things that attract only moths. Hugo admitted that he felt guilty about not selling his coat, but Emmy reassured him that he looked elegant when he wore it.

It was sad that they were living in such destitution. Having arguments about money, confrontations with police, and constant reminders about their poverty, not to mention the restrictions placed upon them and the rest of society as a result of the war. Emmy started to think again that life was hopeless – that things weren't ever going get better. But then, from the silence of the streets, she heard someone singing.

"Listen," Emmy said, pulling Hugo down a side alley. The narrow pathway led into a courtyard, which was filled with brisk, confident music.

"It sounds to me like the piano and drums are crashing against each other," Hugo replied dismissively.

Emmy stood and tried to listen to the lyrics. Then she walked toward the Hotel entrance, where there was an advertisement for a show.

"The Hotel Hirschen is proud to present, the Variété Maxium." Emmy read the sign out loud. On it was a splendid picture of a fire-eater with the words, "Flamingo, King of Magicians." There were a couple of women next to him in the poster who wore tinsel dresses, next to a man who sat low like a frog.

"Let's go inside?" She asked Hugo, who was now a few steps behind her.

"You go ahead," he said. "I'm tired."

"Come on, Hugo. Maybe you'll enjoy it… or maybe there's someone to whom we could sell your coat?"

"I'll wait outside," he said, sitting on a bench.

Emmy nodded, then opened the door just enough to fit inside. She didn't want to leave Hugo, but she had to at least see what was happening. Once she entered, though, she saw the crowd and the lights, and she knew it would be a while longer before she went back outside.

29

Flamingo

Emmy had thought of selling the coat – she really had – but what had happened was, well, she felt a sudden urge to sing on stage again. It had been months since she had the chance or desire, but now she suddenly remembered a song could make life infinitely better.

She recognized the director from the poster outside the hotel. And when she saw him standing at the bar, she walked straight up to him and offered him a proposal. More than she had expected, her sales pitch had worked, and before she knew it, she was singing again.

He directed her to the back, where they gave her a dress to borrow. It was silver lamé and plunged at her neckline. She stood on the stage, exposing all of her voice, breathing in the energy and releasing it back out through the chorus.

She was on the second verse of "La Valse Brune" when she saw Hugo come through the hotel doors. Emmy continued singing as Hugo stood and looked at her silently. Then, through the haze toward the back, she saw that he was smiling.

When the song was over, she turned to the man at the piano and asked him to play one more song. She looked out to Hugo and requested, "Only Love is Life."

***

Needless to say, Emmy was immediately hired. The director even offered her an advance to secure her time in the future. They were a traveling troupe, he had told her, not local from Zurich. He didn't even ask about formal things like paperwork.

Soon, Hugo joined the troupe as well, after the other pianist quit and Emmy suggested him. They traveled together all around Switzerland, from Lake Constance to Basel, crowded together in a gypsy caravan. They had a good time, and they did well enough until the weather got cold and Hugo got sick.

***

"Lousy time," Flamingo said, taking his place in front of the fire. There were ten or twelve of them sitting next to each other, shivering. "But things will look up, not to worry."

Flamingo, the director, whose real name was Ernst Alexander Michael, claimed he was born an actual magician. In his favorite act, which was often the finale, he would light a torch on fire and extinguish it in his mouth.

Flamingo sat next to his wife, Lillymama, who sat next to Hugo – who had been complaining about a toothache and was sleep-deprived and agitated. They were all huddled together at a table in the traditional Swiss restaurant, which had heavy wood paneling in a in the style of a robber baron's castle.

"I'm not sure," Hugo said bitterly. "I'm starting to doubt it. I've lived in Basel before when I was studying. Life has gotten much worse here."

"Why do you say that?" Lillymama asked. She was also a soubrette, like Emmy, and had beautiful brown skin.

"It's like the moral broom of Switzerland here," Hugo said. "They're like the watchful eye of Argus – the giant with one hundred eyes. If they think you don't belong, they'll sweep you back across the border."

Hugo was holding a bag of ice to the side of his mouth. His toothache had lasted now for over a week. Emmy had tried all the home remedies: a saltwater rinse, a cold compress, but not even a cotton ball soaked in morphine seemed to ease his pain. For days, Hugo had stayed in bed feeling sorry for himself, reading Oscar Wilde and Baudelaire. He would only get up to eat or warm up by the fire.

Emmy listened as Hugo kept talking, all the while thinking it wasn't good for his condition.

He told stories from his time at the University of Basel. When he had climbed the spires of the cathedral and watched Professor Nietzsche lecture. The university, he told them, was one of the oldest in the world, known for its library and cross-disciplinary studies. There were classes on everything, from humanities to sciences, but now the campus was different, Hugo claimed. Even the students were more closed-minded and suspicious.

Emmy didn't blame anyone for their judgements. Plus, their little group did look like an unruly lot. They were a collection of the uprooted and addicted and more diverse looking than what most people were familiar with in Switzerland. Of course, people might be suspicious of them, they were unconventional and attention-seeking.

As Hugo continued talking, the tattooed lady got up to retrieve a whistling kettle from the stove. Then, the man whose talent it was to bend like a frog, squatted down in her place with his feet atop the stool. The tight-rope walker was also there, writing quietly in her journal, as well as two acrobats who formerly preformed with the circus.

As a courtesy and, or a way to preserve their sanity, the group tried to avoid talking about current affairs. Hugo was often the one who interjected, which made him, although the most intellectual, the lesser superior among the collective.

Someone passed a bottle of rum, followed by something to smoke, and they all sat half-listening to Hugo's stories until they got tired. The rain drummed down on the roof of their inn, then they quietly ate their dinner and said goodnight.

***

Bum, Bum, Bum, Bum!

It almost sounded like drums, which wouldn't have been so unusual in Basel, except that it wasn't the time of year for carnival. Still, sound wasn't musical. Bum, Bum, Bum, Bum! It was more mechanical, and it was accompanied by loud whistles that rang out through the rainstorm.

Hugo shot up in bed and started searching for something. He pulled the blanket off of Emmy's body.

"What's wrong," she said, suddenly alert. "Is everything okay?"

Hugo was patting the bed down in the dark. His hands moved briskly like he was searching for something to protect them.

Bang, Bang, Bang!

Emmy froze and listened.

"Is it fireworks?" she asked.

"No," Hugo said. He regained some consciousness and got up from the bed. "It's shelling."

Emmy gathered the blanket from off the floor and wrapped it around herself. She stood next to Hugo at the window. In the distance, she saw flashes of light. The sky was dark and filled with low-hanging clouds, but she swore she could see the smoke that rose from the blood.

"They're in Alsace-Lorraine," Hugo said

Emmy knew the region, just a few miles North on the French and German border. It was a fairytale land where the story *Beauty and the Beast* was inspired. There were beautiful timber houses painted in a rainbow of colors, and the vineyards on the rolling hills produced the finest dry Riesling and Gewurztraminer.

"I knew I heard it the other night," Hugo said. "They must have been in Verdun."

It made Emmy a little nervous, being so close to the war, but according to the news reports, they were still safe within the Swiss borders. It was becoming even more difficult now to cross borders, and according to rumors, the bridges were armed with explosives.

"Our neighbors have been at war now for 300 days," Hugo said bleakly. "We have nothing to show for it."

Maybe he was right. Maybe they had been selfish, hiding out in Switzerland. Leaving their family, her daughter, behind. Emmy didn't know what to say. For so long, there was nothing more interesting to her in the world than herself and her fate. Now, she wondered if the right thing to do was stay.

While Emmy was German by birth, she considered herself a mix of nationalities. Danish from her mother's side and French for the language. Parts of her were molded in Moscow and formed in Budapest and other cities like Vienna, which she associated herself with after falling in love there. But now, especially without formal identification, she didn't know if she was from anywhere anymore. For Hugo, however, he remained always German, which remained the one thing that shook the depths of his days.

"It's not even the bad feeling of not being safe in the night," Hugo said. "What I hate is the power and everything that favors it. You don't have to pick up a newspaper to see what power leads to. Look around," Hugo said. "The whole world is falling into nothingness, crying out for magic."

Emmy looked out into the distance, thinking of the soldiers. She wondered if she might be able to sing to the dying, to comfort them.

"I no longer believe in career or money or power," Hugo said. He looked stronger and braver, silhouetted by the low light shining in from the window. "The only thing I believe in now is the powerless and the oppressed."

That, at the least, was their common bond, Emmy thought. Their entire livelihood and peace of mind had been stripped from them because of war. And even though they weren't in the trenches, they were still fighting the same war.

"One cannot love or be saved if they strive to win over their enemies instead of loving them," he said.

That, too, was something Emmy believed in.

She wrapped her arms around Hugo's back and kissed the nape of his neck. "Oh, Hugo," she said. "Can't we play the way we want to live? We are infinitely well. We will never be unhappy again."

30

Mothers, or Love

Emmy never realized how fondly Hugo looked at her until she saw the way he was looking at her in the photo. It was black and white and printed two columns wide, and everyone was smiling into the camera, except for Hugo, who was looking up at her.

She held the newspaper in her hands as she read the review for the "Varieté Maxim" and its "beautiful singer," of whom they were referring to her. In the photo, Emmy was wearing a cream-colored cardigan, buttoned up to her chin, with a satin flower in her hair, which gave her a modest, youthful appearance. She was 30, but could either pass for 20 or 40. Flametti was sitting next to her, in the center of the picture, surrounded by the others, who all looked healthy and happy.

It embarrassed her a little that Hugo was caught showing her so much affection, but then, she thought, she kind of liked that they were getting along so well. The pressures of life had eased a little as the stress of money lessened, and despite life's turmoil they both were happy to live out their passions.

Hugo wasn't exactly optimistic like he was before, but he was more enthusiastic as if he had a plan all along. He had started writing again and had an idea for a novel, he said. He would record his whole philosophy on 200 pages, he told her, and maybe start writing scripts again.

Then, one evening after the show, Emmy was weaving through the tables collecting donations when she saw Flamingo approach Hugo at the piano.

***

"Your little soubrette is quite something," Emmy overheard Flamingo say. "With her talent and your musical directorship, Varieté Maxim is in good hands."

"Thank you," Hugo said as he stood up from the piano. "Everything is exciting and interesting."

Emmy rolled her eyes at Hugo. In her opinion, he and "Ivan the Terrible," were becoming too ambitious. Just that morning, Hugo had to take him to the pharmacy because he had swallowed too much petroleum while practicing a fire trick.

Their eccentric little troupe had started performing Hugo's original titles about Parisian Apaches and widows. Most of the scenes were written without an obvious plot, but Emmy was often in the starring role, so the show was never a flop. With their rhythm and passion, it didn't matter how abstract the message; the intellectuals would pretend to understand, and the others would accept it as entertainment.

Emmy was happy to see Hugo with more energy, but she was surprised by his eager return to theater. After all, he had previously referred to it as a "disheartened puppet show," and she remembered all the times he dismissed her interest in it.

In reality, though, it seemed the overly-critical philosopher was more relaxed with his return to the act. He flourished in Flamingo's little nest, especially together as a couplet.

Emmy was thinking about how Flamingo should give them more money since they were doing so well, but then she saw a pretty older woman come up to Hugo and wrap her arms him. A moment later, she realized it was his mother.

"Darling!" the woman said, reaching her hands to Hugo's face. "It's so nice to see you again."

"Mother…" he stammered, taking a step back. "What are you doing here?"

Emmy stood out of the way but close enough to hear their conversation.

"Well, I think you know the answer to that," she said as she scanned the room with a sense of disgust.

Emmy knew that his mom had threatened to come to Switzerland, but neither she nor Hugo thought she was being serious. Emmy stood silently in shock, then suddenly dropped her basket, sending coins and crumpled notes falling onto the floor.

When Emmy looked up, Hugo was already beside her, helping her pick up the petty cash.

"Mother," he said, giving Emmy his hand. "This is Emmy."

Emmy turned red. "So nice that you're here, Mrs. Ball," she said.

"Yes…" She looked Emmy up and down. "Well, let me assure you, it wasn't the easiest trip."

The woman was wearing an extravagant dress and had a big wool jacket in her arms. She looked longingly at Hugo, who towered over her, and then she turned back to Emmy.

"Hugo talks of you fondly in his letters," she said. "Although, he hasn't told us nearly enough about you."

Hugo looked at Emmy and silently mouthed, "I'm sorry."

"Mother," he said. "How did you get here?"

"I took the train," she said. "I got a passport from your uncle. We all have them now. Well, at least those of us who can afford it. The train was filled with businessmen and honeymooners. Switzerland is quite the destination at the moment."

"You must be exhausted," he said, a bit frazzled. "Here, let me take your coat, mother."

"Oh, Hugo," she said. "This coat is for you, dear. My things are over there by the door." She pointed at the entrance to a stack of luggage.

Emmy thought it was odd that she brought Hugo a coat, then remembered that she liked to sew and wondered if she would make one for her, too.

"…and you, dear," his mother looked at Emmy. "I know you're in costume, but what are you wearing?"

Emmy looked down at herself. She had on a tight dress with a high collar that flattered all the curves of her body. It wouldn't have been offensive necessarily, except that it was a military green and in the style of the French Foreign Legion.

"Do you think it's funny that our brothers are fighting for their adopted country?" Hugo's mother said, somewhat aggressively. "You two should be embarrassed of yourselves. Dressing up like soldiers. You should both be in the trenches with the others. Hugo, don't you know that people call you a traitor back home?"

"A traitor?" Hugo asked. His surprise sounded genuine.

"… and you," she turned to Emmy. "What would you do if you went home and your neighbors threw stones at you?"

Emmy thought for a moment. "Well…" she said. "I supposed I might pick them up and juggle them. I'm pretty good at juggling…"

"Come, Mother," Hugo said, placing his hand firmly on her shoulder. "Let's get you a hotel room and settle down for the night. We can all get to know each other better tomorrow."

***

Hugo's mother only stayed for three days, but by the time she had left, everything had changed.

Hugo became more sensitive and less vulnerable to himself again as if he felt the need to listen to his mother but didn't really want to. The two of them had gotten into numerous heated arguments about whether he should go home and fight in the war. He accused her of wishing he was dead rather than see him happy but poor. Her only clear response was that Germany needed everyone, even if that meant him being at the front line and falling.

"You're right about one thing, mother," he had told her. "Our performances are out of touch with reality. I often think about how our friends in Berlin endure this life. But then, the feeling of enduring enriches and strengthens me. I will be sure to reach out to them and see how they are doing."

Eventually, dramatically, Hugo told his mother to leave. There were other things than war worth dying for, he told her. He said he knew what he wanted and that he wanted to do it. He told her to leave him alone. That his fate was no longer in her hands.

"If you think I'm a coward," he told her, "you're wrong."

Emmy felt sad for his mother, even if the woman had never attempted to be kind to her. Even when Emmy would try to show her how hard she was working, the woman continued to judge otherwise. Still, Emmy could understand where she was coming from. A mother's love was flawed, if not vulnerable and pure. She knew she would be sad, too, if her daughter dismissed her.

31

Resolutions

As the year came to a close, so did the show in Basel, and the next city on their tour just happened to be Zurich. By mid-December, they were back where they once felt at home, with the same friendly faces and cobblestone alleys.

In proper Zurich fashion, the city was bustling with energy. There was a sense of holiday magic in the nearly frozen air. The warm smell of roasted chestnuts rose from the street stalls and the snow-topped mountains peaked out from the far side of the lake.

They spent Christmas together as a troupe. Flamingo, the father for all of them. He gave each of them a gift on Christmas morning; Hugo a typewriter, and Emmy a book of 1,000 short stories she had never read before.

But while the end of the year had given Emmy a sense of closure, she wasn't exactly feeling as steady as she had hoped. Every day, life was still a test of endurance, just as it was for those in the war.

Night after night, they performed at every venue in Niederdorf, the locals attending each evening in droves. But during the day, they would lose their way, with thoughts about how they could better serve the world.

Hugo was still deep in guilt for his country. And to cope, he threw himself into the literary scene, exploring his ideas. He spent most days at the library, where only men were allowed, and so Emmy was often home alone with her vices and thoughts in her head.

She didn't have anyone to blame for her restlessness except maybe Hugo's mother. Ever since she had visited, she started to question her own role as one – and everything she had done wrong. She wondered if she'd been selfish and if that were bad. She thought about how she had left behind both her son and her daughter but never truly repented.

She tried to write about her past as a way to cope, but reliving her history only made her feel worse. She could feel herself on the verge of another breakdown but told herself she didn't have time to be. Instead, she tried to stay loyal to her hope and to Hugo, as if they were facing a riddle that they could only solve together.

***

Emmy held Hugo's hand like a child as they left the small, old-fashioned inn. They had been at the Hollandische Meierei, at Spiegelgasse 1, around the corner from where they had once lived.

"It was a good show," Emmy said, tired but proud of what they had accomplished. She pulled Hugo close to her body for warmth and comfort.

"I suppose," he replied.

Emmy looked at him. Snowflakes fell into his eyes.

"What's wrong?" she asked.

"I don't know," he said. "I just want to do something different."

"Like what?"

"I'm not sure," he said. "I just feel the need to disappear more and more into this little life. Obtain a new form of freedom and have our own ensemble. Write it."

"Have our own theater?" Emmy considered it.

She had been young and naive when she had first started to perform, wearing fairytale dresses with her hair in blonde curls. Now though, even though she enjoyed it, she was starting to become more jaded about the theater herself.

"I want to be a role model for a younger generation," Hugo said. "One who will be liberal but not politically active. Like the Hamburgische Dramaturgie. Have you heard of them?"

"No…" Emmy said.

"It's a series of essays from the 1760s," he said. "It argues that theater's role as a vehicle for the advancement of humanistic discourse. Take Aristotle and his theory of tragedy. The emotional response he creates among the audience is the perfect example. Just when we reach the point where we think we are justified in boldness and wrongdoing, the dramatist in all of us divides, not at a loss for final motivation."

Emmy remembered her nights at the Simplicissimus, her days in Munich when she first met Hugo, and how she was always circled by writers, artists and friends. When everything was beautiful, and everything was good.

"Like the Simplicissimus?" Emmy asked, starting to get excited.

"Yes," Hugo replied, smiling, "…but more artistic and intentional."

"Okay," Emmy agreed. "But where will we perform?"

"I've already got that covered," Hugo said. "I've requested renting the space from Mr. Ephran."

"The owner of the Merei?" Emmy asked.

"Sure," Hugo said. "He told me himself it would be the perfect place for an artists' bar. He even said that he's had poetry readings there before."

Emmy tried to imagine Hugo's vision. It wasn't an artist's bar. It was a run-down pub that was dark and smelled of sausages. The lamps were covered in dull-red cloths that emitted an ominous light, and the tables were covered in red-checkered tablecloths with baskets of hard-boiled eggs in the middle. And the worst part about it, Emmy thought, was that the guests would be eating while they watched the performance. She imagined their own show might be more …intimate.

"What will you call it?"

He thought for a moment.

"The Cabaret Voltaire," he replied. "After the French enlightener."

It had a nice ring to it.

"It will be our '*Candide ou l'optimisme,*'" Hugo replied. "That life is worth living."

ACT III

The Cabaret Voltaire

Zurich, Switzerland
February, 1916

32

Optimism (the Philosophy)

"Wolken"

"elomen, elomen, lefitalominai"

Emmy stood over Hugo, who was sitting at his desk reading out the words from his machine.

"wolminuscaio, baumbala bunga, acycam glastula feirofim flinsi…"

She turned her head slightly, looked at him critically, and wondered if he was still sane.

"Do you need help?" she asked. "I'm not sure you've hit the right keys."

"No," Hugo said. "I know what I'm doing."

He continued typing, then looked up at her, removing the paper from the machine.

"Here," he said. "Read it aloud."

"Gaga, oo, bimba," she tried to use the right pronunciation, but the words were all rubbish. They didn't make sense.

"Not like that," Hugo said, taking the paper back. "Now, listen to me."

"Endremin, saassa, flumen, flobollala, fellobash, falljada, follidi."

As he began reading, she noticed the difference. There was a rhythm to his voice but in a spirit of improvisation. It was experimental, almost like putting jazz into verse.

"It's just clouds," he said. "Cats and peacocks. But it's not about the words."

Emmy raised her eyebrow and smiled at him, showing her support. She wasn't sure anyone would like it, but that's what progress was, she thought: innovation.

***

In the days that followed, Hugo and Emmy put their plan into action, gathering their team and preparing the troops. They sent letters to all their friends asking them to join.

"Send us interesting people so we can achieve something beautiful," they wrote. "Please send a picture, a drawing, an engraving. We would like to combine a small exhibition with our cabaret."

Hugo wrote to Hans Arp, an artist he knew from Munich. "He's also living in Switzerland to avoid the war," he told Emmy. "He's French but born in Strasbourg, which makes him a German citizen by conquest."

He also wrote to Richard Huelsenbeck, the musician and writer whom Emmy had met at the Commemoration of the Fallen Poets. As well as to Frank Wedekind, whom Emmy had heard was now married and living monogamously.

Emmy wrote to Rudi, Hardy, Else and Lotte, inviting them to send their artwork and come in person if ever possible. She also wrote to Erich but asked him not to send anything too radical.

Along with their friends, they invited the public. Hugo typed up an announcement to be printed in the papers.

"Young artists of Zurich," he wrote in the ad, "whatever their orientation, are invited to come along with suggestions and contributions of all kinds."

It would be an open stage, he decided, without much directing. They didn't know who might show up or how it would go.

It all made Hugo excited, and Emmy a little nervous.

***

With the venue secured and the press invited, the next step was to set the stage. Mr. Ephraim committed to leasing the space for five nights a week, and he led them up a narrow flight of stairs into a dusty, dark room.

"It's just the perfect place for an artist bar!" he said. "Don't you agree?"

Emmy looked around. The Meierei didn't quite meet her idea of an intimate space with velvet curtains and good lighting.

"We held poetry readings here last fall."

Emmy looked at Hugo.

"Is there electricity?" Hugo asked.

"Sure," the man said. He was tall and had a mustache. "There's an outlet in the back. No toilet, though."

"Thank you, Mr. Ephram, we appreciate it greatly."

Emmy rolled her eyes.

"My pleasure," he said, looking at her. "Just remember, no 'Tingle Tangle,' and don't disturb the neighbors."

Emmy waited until the landlord left, then asked Hugo, "Are you sure?"

"It will be great," he replied. "It will be perfect."

***

That evening, they began their work to create their cabaret, in which they planned to integrate all forms of art and create new forms of expression. Emmy sat down on the wooden floor, which was worn and splintered. She dipped a brush into a can of paint and then dragged it above the baseboard. It felt a bit heavy like it held all her fears, but it slid across the wall easily, like it was something it was meant for.

She looked over at Hugo, who was trying to get a piano up the stairs with Arp. A task as vulnerable and dangerous as the people who were managing it.

She wasn't necessarily afraid of Hugo's plan, but she thought she knew better than he how difficult and painful life could be when it came to art. She put down her brush, reached into her pocket and took a sip of morphine from the small glass jar.

She painted the walls a deep, sensual blue, which perhaps added to her sense of growing vulnerability. She missed her friends back in Germany, and she was upset that she hadn't received a reply from anyone she had written to yet.

Hugo's letters, on the other hand, were answered almost immediately – and with enthusiastic responses, thriving with excitement. Arp – who went by "Jean" when speaking French – even arrived early, offering to help prepare the cabaret.

Emmy watched the men position the piano in the center of the stage, and then Hugo slid a bench across the floor and sat down to play. With one note, then two, his fingers floated over the keys, filling the room with music. A warm, soothing energy.

"Can I help?"

Emmy looked up from her daze and found Arp standing beside her. "Oh, sure," she replied. "If you'd like." She handed him a paint roller and tray.

"So…" he said as Hugo's song played in the background. "How do you like Switzerland?"

She thought about it for a minute. "What is there not to like?" she said. "It's like a fairytale here."

"It is, isn't it?" he replied enthusiastically. "It's paradisiacal, really, almost like the rest of the world doesn't exist."

Emmy nodded. "Yes," she said. "If we didn't hear stories of what was happening, it would be easy to forget it."

"What brought you to Zurich?"

"Same thing as you, I suppose."

Arp nodded. "The Swiss Alps are a good place to hide from a war. Have you been to Ticino yet? In the Italian side of Switzerland?"

"No." She shook her head.

"Oh, you have to go. There's an artists' retreat on the side of a mountain. I met my girlfriend, Sophie, there at Monte Verità. She was training with a group of dancers under the teacher, Laban. They call him the 'pioneer of modern' dance because he believes rhythm comes from the body, not the music. Or, at least, that's what Sophie tells me. He has a school here in Zurich as well, but at his summer school in Ticino, which is perched over a great lake, they all eat vegetarian food and take 'air baths' naked in the sun.

Emmy was intrigued, and she found the man enjoyably funny. "How do you know Hugo, exactly?"

"Oh," Arp replied. "I met him when we were both in Munich. I believe he was preparing for the production of a play. We also have some mutual friends: Hans Richter, Erich Mühsam…"

"Oh!" Emmy smiled at the mention of Erich's name. Then she remembered how Hans had declared Hugo a "brilliant and genius director" and that one could expect something "beautiful and great" from him one day.

"Hugo!" Arp yelled over toward the piano. "What play were you directing when we met?"

Hugo looked toward them, his hands still gliding across the piano keys. "*Das Leben das Menschen*," he said. "The one Emmy was going to star in."

He was right, Emmy remembered. They never did the play.

"It was just before the draft," Hugo said, getting up from the piano mid-note and walking toward them. "When everyone was leaving for war."

"Yes," Arp said. "That was it. Have I ever told you how I avoided the draft, by the way?"

Hugo and Emmy shook their heads.

"You know how you have to fill out a paper with all your information? Well... instead of writing my name and address in the blanks, I wrote down random numbers and added them all up at the end. Then, when I had to report for duty, I submitted my paperwork in the nude."

"You did not!" Emmy exclaimed.

"You did?" Hugo asked.

Hans shrugged and said in French, "They do not want crazy people in war."

"I suppose that's true," Emmy said, in somewhat disbelief. "But who's to say who's crazy and who isn't."

"You know..." Hans said, rolling the deep blue paint over the wall. "I believe art can heal people from the madness of our times."

Emmy nodded. "I feel the same way about songs."

"Painting, writing, composing, the activity of any art would do everyone good," Hugo replied. "Provided they do not pursue any purpose in their subjects."

"The law of chance," Hans suggested.

"Exactly," Hugo said. "Follow the course of a free, unfettered imagination."

"Whoever follows this law will create pure life," Hans said, playing off of Hugo's direction. Then, he took a step back to admire the freshly-painted room.

"Oh, here," he said, walking over to a suitcase lying on the floor. "I brought you some art. There's an O.

van Rees, an Arthur Segal and a sketch by Pablo Picasso."

"Wonderful!" Hugo replied, walking over to get a closer look. "I saw a Picasso once in Dresden at an exhibition for futurist painters. It was a lively place."

"And this one?" Emmy asked, pointing to a different sketch.

"This one I did myself," Arp replied. "Black ink over pencil on paper, in pure, geometric form."

"It's beautiful," Emmy said.

"Yes," Hugo agreed. "Abstract… like doing away with sentences for the sake of the individual word."

They all shook their heads in agreement and smiled, admiring the art.

33

Opening night

On opening night, the place was jammed. With two hours to showtime it was already nearly standing room only.

They were all still working frantically to finish the last preparations. Hugo was tuning the piano, and Arp was nailing masks and posters to the wall. Emmy, not yet in her dress, was taping opaque paper to the windows that faced the alley.

A few small tables in the middle of the room were circled with people. The larger tables had been pushed against the wall, and groups of students were drinking at the round ones in the middle. Emmy recognized some of their faces from the Russian dining hall, but others were unfamiliar and spoke in unusual dialects.

"Excuse me…" a foreign voice sounded out from behind Emmy. She turned around but didn't recognize the man, nor the three others he was with.

"My name is Tristan Tzara," he said, offering his hand.

He was short and dapper and wore a monocle under his right eye. He shook Emmy's hand and kissed the top of it.

"Marcel Janco," the tall one said next, practically pushing the short one aside. "And this is my brother, Georges, and…"

Emmy tried to place their accent. They all had dark hair, tan skin, and were handsome.

"Nice to meet you," she said. She wondered where they came from.

Hugo, who had finished with the piano, came over toward Emmy, who was now circled by the men.

"Excuse me," he said, eyeing them critically. "We're not quite ready, as you can see. But if you come back in a few hours…"

"No, no," the tall one replied. Then he said something to the others, which Emmy couldn't understand.

Arp, who was standing nearby hanging posters, was also drawn into the conversation, which was growing louder.

"What do they want?" he asked Hugo.

Hugo shook his head. "I don't know.

"Maybe they want to perform," Emmy said.

"Da!" The one in the middle replied, shaking his head.

"Yes, we mean," Tzara said. "Perform. Me, a poem, and my friend, Janco, a magnificent painting." They each held out their treasures like the Three Wise Men.

"Oh," Hugo said, almost embarrassedly. "Yes, of course! You must have seen the announcement in the paper. We'd be happy to have you at the Cabaret Voltaire."

The tall one smiled and handed Hugo a painting.

"I call it *Archangels*," he said.

***

By the time Hugo took the stage, all the seats were filled. The room was loud, but it had an intimate feel. Emmy stood off the stage, waiting for Hugo to begin. She still had some apprehension, but she fully trusted him.

Hans Richter was right. She thought in the moments before going on stage. If anyone deserved to be famous, then it was Hugo. It was his moment to shine. It was he who was ready to be recognized for his genius.

With a slight shake in his voice, Hugo thanked the audience for coming, and then he took a seat at the piano and slowly began to play. Emmy took a deep breath and walked onto the stage. Then, at Hugo's mark, she sang.

The hypnotic sound of a French love song could charm anyone. At least, that's what she told Hugo when she suggested she open with it. She moved her body rhythmically from side to side, in sync with the risqué French chanson in traditional keys. Her brassy hair reflected the light. The room was silent.

Emmy looked at the audience and noticed that their silhouettes were also moving to the rhythm of the melody. The brightest light came from the back alley, which created a glowing outline around their landlord, who was swaying in the doorway.

As the song came to an end, Emmy slid down to the floor with her legs stretched out on each side.

The crowd erupted louder than she had ever heard before, and then Hugo, building on their energy, began playing an improvised, upbeat number with atypical patterns.

"Ms. Emmy Hennings!" Hugo yelled into the crowd. Emmy bowed and smiled, then walked off the stage as Hugo welcomed a man named Rudolf Anders in her place.

Emmy was sweating, and her heart was racing, but for the first act, she thought it was a positive reaction. She stood off the stage and gathered her breath as she watched the man read his poem. He, too, had seen the announcement in the paper and came to share his work.

After him, a woman named Miss Riesa Helm sang a Danish song while Hugo stayed on the piano. Emmy, who knew the song from her childhood, winced when the woman hit the wrong note and joined in during the chorus to compliment her.

After intermission, Hugo recited a poem by the French surrealist Rimbaud about a boat that breaks free of human society. Then, the man named Tzara took the stage. He fumbled with pieces of paper that he retrieved one-by-one from the depths of his pockets. He looked dapper, Emmy thought, but also slightly helpless. For a moment, she thought she would have to save him, too, but then he began speaking in his native tongue, which sounded like a strange, captivating rain of words.

At the end of his poem, Tzara bowed politely. The audience was charmed. They all clapped and stood up from their chairs, swooning like they were in love.

Emmy was impressed and watched as Hugo kept playing a swing tune to keep the cheers from overflowing. Then, Tzara left the stage as if Hugo was directing him.

At the end of the show, Hugo stood up and thanked everyone for coming. But as he bowed, a man cried out: "It is war! Fraternizing is forbidden!"

The audience got quiet, but then someone started booing, and others started laughing. Hugo winked at Arp, who was standing in the back laughing. If the act had been pre-directed, they had forgotten to tell Emmy.

Then, as if they were all family, everyone in the room cheered and drank the last sips of their beer.

The show was a hit, Emmy decided as she looked out onto the crowd. Hugo's cabaret was an overnight sensation.

34

Dance of the Death

Performances continued until the end of February, five nights a week, just as they had promised. The reviews in the newspapers weren't sure how to describe them. They were praised for offering new acts every evening, but were called "nihilists," which suggested they didn't stand for anything.

It was true that each night that they performed they never really had a plan. Hugo might read a translated poem from Kandinsky or play an improved piano tune. Emmy would read some words of her own or do a little dance. And Arp, who was also a regular, would often read something he wrote while sitting intimately, cross-legged on the floor.

When they would receive a piece of art from a friend or acquaintance, they would add it to the rotation. Else sent a poem and Wedekind offered his *Thunder Song*, which was powerfully read by one of the men.

Tzara, Huelsenbeck and Janco were also always in the show, as well as a 20-man Russian Balalaika band, who had begged to be regulars. They showcased works by Christian Morgenstern, Jakob van Hoddis, Oskar Kokoschka and Alfred Lichtenstein. And eventually, Emmy and Hugo even performed *The Life of Man*.

Hugo was immediately drawn to the dreamless expanse, always coming up with unusual acts and suggestions. And for the most part, Emmy went along with his plan without protest. She didn't worry about their reputation or that one might not find meaning to their irregular acts, though, lately, she was beginning to feel a bit exhausted.

That day, for example, before the show, she had to work the cloakroom, collect tickets, search for a cash register and iron Hugo's suit and tie. Then, she had to meet a singer and a dancer who wanted to rehearse – all before 8 p.m., when the next show began. On top of the tasks that kept her busy with work, she kept having a strange dream about her grandmother, which she felt was some kind of warning.

Emmy stood behind the counter and pushed the coats aside. If she took her grandmother's warnings seriously though, all her efforts would be in vain. She had stopped reading the newspaper for the same reason, she determined. Worrying about everything in the world would just make someone sick to their stomach.

She reached into her coat pocket and pulled out a small mirror. Thirty-one wasn't so old, she thought, but the morphine always had made her look colorless and left dark circles under her eyes.

She removed a small bag from her purse on the counter, then sat on the floor and began to put make-up on. Soon, the bags under her eyes were hidden by a thick circle of coal. She painted her face white and made her lips bright red to represent death.

"Are you ready?" Hugo asked, bringing in another coat and hanging it on the rack.

"Almost," Emmy said, putting away her things, even though she wasn't sure she was, really. It felt as if she was climbing out of a dark hole and was too tired to get out. But she wouldn't tell Hugo that, even if she was. He held enough of the world's heavy worries to worry about hers.

She stood up, her face painted like a corpse, then put the mirror back in her coat pocket and removed the bottle of Morphine. Just a sip sent her back to that quiet spot, where a colorful world of otherness slowly unfolded around her.

She noticed Hugo looking at her from the corner of her eye, giving her a concerned look of surprise. He didn't say anything, though, and so she went to change into her costume.

***

On stage, Emmy stood in a silk skirt and topaz-green sweater. She faced the audience with an exasperated gaze but full of burning being.

She waited for Hugo's direction, then his hands took the lead. A key, then another, as the whispers and chatter from the audience deceased. Hugo looked over his shoulder and smiled at Emmy. Then, in a trembling voice, she began to sing.

"In the morning, still in sleep and dream,
at noon already there,
evenings in the grave.
That's how we die, that's how we die,
that's how we die every day.
Because he makes it so easy to die."

The room was completely silent, the audience focused on Emmy. Then, Hugo started banging on the piano, which made them all jump with surprise.

With his cue, Emmy began to twitch, shaking her chest and bending her arms and legs out of place. She convulsed violently like she was possessed, then three men sang out behind her in unison.

"So we murder, so we kill,
So we murder every day

Our comrades in the dance of death...

We do not grumble, we do not growl,
We are silent all days...
We thank you, we thank you,
Mr. Kaiser for the grace.
That you have chosen us to die."

Emmy closed her eyes for the third verse. She sang softly as if she was vanishing suddenly and completely.

"Sleeping only, sleepy and quiet.
Until you are resurrected
Our poor body that covers the lawn."

The audience stayed quiet as if they didn't know how to react.

Then, Mr. Ephran turned on the lights, and the room broke out in applause.

***

After the dance, Emmy brushed her hand across her face, leaving smears of white make-up across her wrist as she walked off the stage.

In the audience were the usual guests. The students in their dapper hats and half-empty cups of cold *café crème.* But there were new faces, too, she noticed. Couples in elegant outfits dressed up like they belonged somewhere nicer – like in Corso, the new theater that opened near the Opera House. The Cabaret Voltaire, it seemed, was becoming popular with the rich and famous. What she didn't notice, however, was that as she walked between the tables, everyone seemed to move closer together.

"You did great," Hugo said, coming up beside her.

"I don't know," she replied. "You don't think the despair and hopelessness was too much?"

"No," Hugo replied. "Besides, it's not the words of the song that matter. The laws of rhythm are more important. It's not ABAB or CDDC, but DADA, which upsets the reader's expectations.

She stood and looked at him with her corpse face.

"Anyway," he said, "People prefer melody to the word."

Emmy nodded. It wasn't that she cared what anyone thought. She had been judged her whole life. First, for how pretty she was, and then for how talented. If they knew anything else about her life, she thought, she would also be judged for it.

"Emmy," Hugo said. "I'm worried about you, though. Maybe it was the dance or the make-up, but you're looking a little lost and gone."

"What do you mean?" she replied angrily. "I'm fine." How could he accuse her? She had been holding it all together for him. Doing all the work.

"Maybe you should take a break," he said. "Get out of bed before the sun falls."

"Nothing is wrong," she said, even though she knew he could sense it. She didn't talk about the sunshine or delight in life's surprises anymore. It was as if she was waiting for a new adventure, but the days just piled higher. She could only push through life unsteadily and sleep until it was over.

"I'm fine, Hugo," she said. "Really."

Then, she took her coat off the rack and walked out the door.

35

A Change of Scene, or Men

It was snowing, and it was cold. The weather was heavy with gray clouds of winter. Emmy's eyes teared up as she walked, but neither she nor anyone else could tell if her eyes dripped from the wind or her sorrows.

A narrow alley alongside the cabaret led up to a cobblestone courtyard. In the middle stood a fountain with icicles hanging like daggers from the mouths of cast-iron angels. Men were smoking cigarettes on the benches nearby and looked up at Emmy as she passed them. One looked her straight in the eye, but she quickly turned away so he wouldn't ask how she was doing.

She knew some people in life subordinated themselves to the opinions of others, but she could say confidently this was not the case for herself. Hugo never used drugs. He claimed a sip of alcohol was enough to make him sick. The only thing he could sometimes enjoy, he told her, was the sparkling Sekt of strawberry punch. Still, it wasn't as if his appearance was any better than hers. He wasn't sleeping either, and he was also overworked.

At the back of the courtyard, the cobblestones led down a small hill, where she found a seat on a bench in a small park circled by trees. As she sat down, brushing aside the snow, she reached into her pocket for the small glass bottle and held it safely in her hand.

She took in a deep breath and looked around. The snow was falling slowly, and her breath froze in the air. A pair of lovers in the alley slowly walked by arm in arm, then stopped under a streetlamp to kiss lovingly.

It was useless, she knew, to judge anyone's being, but she couldn't help but to want to place herself in their moment. She may not care what others thought of her, but she still wanted everyone to love her.

A light went on in a window above where the couple was standing and she saw a man staring down at her. He was thin and bald with a thick mustache and goatee, and he radiated the same seriousness of Hugo's being. Emmy stared back at him, not wanting to be the first to break contact, but then she realized he was actually looking into his own reflection. He stood by the window for another minute or two, then sat down at a desk, which she could see was piled with books.

Emmy watched as the man in the window bent over a typewriter and frantically began typing. He raised his head less often as time passed, completely absorbed by his work.

Emmy thought about what might come out of her thoughts if she sat down to write them so eagerly. She, too, wanted to be absorbed by something as passionately as this man, but for the first time, she wasn't sure if she was living for love or work.

***

The next night, Emmy went to the cabaret despite Hugo's advice to stay at home. Why confine herself to her bed and her thoughts, she debated, when instead she could express Hugo's thoughts through her art?

She was lying on top of a long bench that protruded slightly from a wooden table. One leg was bent, the other stretched out in front of her as she counted the white spots she had missed in the ceiling, forming a constellation in her black sky.

"Hi, Emmy," Tzara said, coming up to sit beside her. "What are you doing?" He gently pushed her leg to the side so he could have more room.

"Nothing," Emmy said, swinging her legs around the bench, her silk dress sliding down her thigh. She looked at Tzara. He was young, not yet 20, and had a face that was still round with baby fat. Hugo wasn't particularly fond of him, but Emmy didn't mind him.

For how modest Hugo was, Tzara was the opposite. He was precocious beyond his years, and spoke in such beautiful syllables.

"Are you ready for tonight?" he asked, adjusting his monocle.

"Sure," she said. "I'm always ready." What she didn't tell him was that she was longing for an abysmal change. That she wanted to go her own way but was uncertain to where and with whom. That even though she knew the reason was inside her, that change seemed unfathomable.

"Good," he said. "Me too."

***

That night, Emmy sang while Tzara, Janco, Huelsenbeck, and Arp shouted obscure sighs of love, moos, and meowing behind her. Then, Tzara, who was dressed in a dapper two-piece suit, started shaking his rear end, which drove all the women crazy. He swayed back and forth like an oriental dancer while Janco pretended to play the violin, and then, to end it all, Emmy did the splits.

"It was total pandemonium!" Arp exclaimed as they walked off the stage. The three of them were sweating, and the audience was cheering.

"Emmy!"

"Emmy!"

People were calling her name, but when she looked around, she didn't recognize any of them.

"It's like a cosmopolitan mixture of God and brothel in here," Tzara said, coming up beside her.

"What is that supposed to mean?" Emmy asked, looking at his hand on her shoulder.

"This place," he said. "The energy." He spun around smiling, then headed into the crowd.

"Miss Hennings?" A man appeared next to her. "Excuse me. I'm a reporter for the paper. Can I speak to you for a moment?"

Emmy took a step back to look at the man and found him strikingly handsome.

"Can I get you a drink? I have a couple of questions for you."

"… sure," Emmy said, wondering what it was that he wanted.

"Emmy! Emmy!" She kept hearing her name, but then, she thought, maybe it was just a voice in her head. She weaved through the crowd, following the journalist, who turned around a few times to say something that she couldn't understand.

She looked around for a familiar face but didn't see Hugo, Tzara, or Mr. Ephram. As they made their way to the bar, she thought of what she might say.

"Here you go," the man said, handing her a tall glass.

"Thanks," she said, loud enough for him to hear over the crowd. "Sorry, what did you say your name was?"

"Vayo," he replied with a Spanish accent, moving closer to her ear. She felt his breath on her neck and smelled notes of patchouli.

"Hi," she murmured as if she was under a spell. "Nice to meet you…"

"I wanted to ask you…"

"What?" she couldn't hear him. The chatter and clatter of the Balalaika Band had spilled into the crowd.

"I wanted to ask you," he said, his cheek grazing hers, "about the show… how did you…"

Suddenly, Emmy felt a hand on her back. She froze and looked up, locking eyes with Hugo.

"Emmy," he said. "Let's go."

Her heart started to race. She wanted to say no, but then she smiled politely at the man and got up to leave with Hugo.

***

After that night, Hugo started to complain of the "undefined ecstasy" that seemed to have taken hold of everybody. The small cabaret had burst at its seams, he said, and was "escalating into a playground of crazy emotions." He warned the others that Mr. Ephram was complaining about the noise and debauchery and that they would have to change their act if they wanted to survive.

He called for more diversity, less emotion, and more seriousness. He orchestrated special soirees for works by the French, Russian, and Swiss. He didn't include a German evening because that could be considered "political propaganda," even though the other languages also belonged to wartime nations. Every night, artists from a single nation now performed to showcase their culture, but the result was just different combinations of old and new music. A few amateur poets, awkward and nervous, performed to an audience that had come seeking the notorious exaltation, and now often left disappointed.

Emmy favored the sensual performances of a traditional cabaret, even if they were sometimes interpreted as overly suggestive. She didn't worry that Hugo might be jealous because there was nothing to be jealous of. Still, he seemed to be more agitated with her than before, but Emmy brushed the feeling away. Even things that were serious and true, she knew, could often be deceiving.

Instead, she let Hugo work and talk about richness and propaganda. He questioned whether words, music, art, or anything really mattered. He was frustrated that his theories weren't understood by the audience and the press. He claimed everyone was blind to misguided information. It didn't matter what something was called, he wanted to shout. It was simply about the act that was happening, he repeated over and over again.

One night, at the end of a rather dull show, a group of Dutch boys arrived, acting like complete fools. They had banjos and mandolins and called themselves *Oily Knee*. And Mr. Oily Knee, the lead performer, yelled into the crowd, "Follow me!" Up on the stage, he did a crazy dance. Twisting, bending, and shaking with eccentric steps. Then, in an act of pure riot, he led the audience onto the street, chanting loudly into the night.

36

More Drums

From then on, whether Hugo wanted it or not, the Cabaret Voltaire played and raised hell. There were cowbells, drums, yells, blows, and wild accents. And eventually, Mr. Ephram really did start to get upset.

"A police report!" their landlord yelled, slamming a paper onto the table where Tzara, Hugo, Emmy, Arp, and Janco were all sitting. They had been trying to come up with a name for their new singer, and they looked up in surprise when he cut them off so furiously.

"A police report?" Hugo asked in a sincere, surprised tone. "For what?" He sprung up from the table and went out with Mr. Ephraim to discuss the problem in private.

"*Madame Le Roy* is too formal," Tzara said, thumbing through a dictionary, unconcerned with Hugo's issue. He looked up at the woman fondly as the red light from the table lamp illuminated her chestnut skin.

Their new singer was striking; even Emmy thought so, and Tzara was right. Her name was too formal.

"D.." Tzara said. "D…Da… Dach… Dachziegel... Dafür... " He slid his finger down the German words in the book. "Dame?"

"What does it mean?" the woman asked shyly.

"A noble lady," he replied, which made her giggle.

Emmy sat cross-legged on the bench across from them, watching them flirt. Then, she remembered the handsome journalist and wondered if he would come back or if Hugo had scared him away for good. She wanted to answer his questions and ask some about him too, for example, where he came from and what adventures he had been on.

"A noise violation!" Hugo said, coming back to the table. He held the paper in his hand and waved it in the air.

"A noise violation? Who cares?" Tzara waved him off. "We're putting on a show. Anyway, Janco trades opium here illegally."

Janco shook his head. "Wait, what? No, I don't."

Tzara laughed and removed his monocle to wink at the woman.

"Don't be fooled," Janco told her. "He is an excellent organizer and vindictive self-promoter, but not truly a man of culture."

Suddenly, the back door flew open with a rush of frozen air, and a man's silhouette appeared in the flurry of snow.

They all turned to look at him as he yelled, "We're going to need more drums!"

**

Intentional or not, Hugo's resolve to keep an open mind meant that the cabaret performances got weirder and wilder. His invitation to let everyone perform, no matter who they were, meant that anyone could come onto the stage without poise or discretion.

When Richard Huelsenbeck arrived, though, with his kettledrum in arms, Hugo's direction changed again. It seemed he was no longer worried about the noise.

His goal, again, was to provide a center for artistic entertainment. Policing someone's creativity would be like a general justifying his actions, Hugo said to them all after Huelsenbeck had arrived.

"The only difference," he said, "was the government uses political jargon to protect their stale ideas. *They* were going to do the opposite; remove all meaning."

Emmy wasn't sure what Hugo meant exactly, but she could see that Huelsenbeck's arrival had sparked something in him. Almost immediately, his desire to please was replaced with the desire to experiment again. He started talking about how entertainment didn't matter. That one must confront the popular narrative through brutish music and new verse.

Emmy remembered how passionately Huelsenbeck had spoken at the "Commemoration of the Fallen Poets," in Berlin, which Hugo had hosted before they left for Zurich. But she also remembered not quite understanding everything he was saying. He had a college-boy insolence, which Hugo seemed charmed by, but turned other people were turned off by him, especially Tzara. Still, he immediately became a driving force in their troupe. A fresh, intellectual bang against the backdrop of war.

The war, Huelsenbeck had explained the night he arrived, was the same old news of destruction and death. Emmy no longer read the newspapers, but it was clear that Switzerland was seeing more action — not because of their own citizen, but those who were coming into the country. Prisoners of war, the walking wounded, young men who, like Huelsenbeck, faced death saving their country. They streamed into their dear *Helvetia* in rows, whether their nationality was French, Austrian, Russian, or German.

Huelsenbeck had come directly from Munich with stories of their homeland. He talked for hours about the economy, which he said had crashed, along with the British blockade of foreign goods, which had left thousands of people starving. The food was almost as scarce as the men, he told them, and he said it had been years since he had broken bread.

He recounted how he served in the war but never made it to the front because of his neuralgia. He described repetitively how the pain pulsed like electric shocks through the nerves in his face, but how he was also grateful for it.

It was only by the grace of God, he had told them, that he had escaped the blood ocean that was now Germany.

37

Ghosts

The next day was Sunday, which meant there was no show, which would have been the perfect day to stay in bed, except Emmy was craving a croissant. Rich, buttery layers of freshly baked dough. She was ashamed of the desire she had felt after Huelsenbeck's report from Germany. There, Huelsenbeck had told them, their friends and families suffered from a harsh winter. Peasants and horses were recruited for war, and the alternative to bread was potato starch enriched with sawdust.

Emmy felt sad for her friends, who were only just a few hours away by train. It was never fair when some people suffered while others flourished. She prayed for them, sending warm thoughts and blessings. Then she got out of bed and got dressed to go to the bakery.

It was the only sensible thing to do in a situation like this, Emmy believed. One could only do what they could with love and be open to the next perfect day to arrive.

Emmy waited in line at the bakery, thinking about butter, when the man in front of her stepped back accidentally bumping into her.

She looked at him for a moment, remembering his face, then he smiled and said, "Miss Hennings," in a Spanish accent.

"Vayo," Emmy said shyly. Her heart started to race and she could feel herself turning red.

"The angel of the Cabaret Voltaire," he said. "What a lucky game of chance to see you here."

Emmy blushed. "I'm sorry about the other night," she said, remembering their abrupt departure. "There's just so much going on after each show, and…"

"No need to apologize," he explained. "I'm just glad to have the opportunity to speak to you again."

"Can I help you?" the lady behind the counter asked in the local dialect.

"Yes, please," Vayo responded seamlessly. "Two loaves of bread." The woman looked at him, then at Emmy, as she told him the price. He handed her the coins then turned back to Emmy.

"Here," he said, offering her the bigger of the two loaves. "This is for you."

She took the bread into her arms like a baby. It was still warm and smelled of love and safety.

"I have to go," he said. "I have an appointment, but can I see you soon? I want to ask you about the show and your vision."

Emmy didn't quite know what to say, but before she could say no, he took her hand and kissed the back of it.

"Sunset," he suggested. "At the lake."

"Sunset," Emmy repeated, then looked at the bread. "Thank you."

He smiled, then left.

Emmy was overwhelmed by the thought of the man. He was handsome and tall and had a deep, alluring accent. The whole way home, she remained lost in her daydream, so much so that she didn't even check the mailbox as she normally did.

***

Once Hugo woke up, they ate the bread, which was sweet on its own without any jam. Then Hugo confessed that he forgot to tell Emmy that he had invited everyone to their apartment to work.

Huelsenbeck arrived shortly after with his drum. Then Arp, and his Swiss girlfriend, Sophie, who carried a stack of magazines in her arms. Janco came too, and then their one-room apartment on Predigerplatz quickly turned into a circus tent. Emmy watched in bewilderment as they all worked toward a common goal, unsure if they really knew what their goal was.

Hugo was working on a suit of sorts, painted silver and made of a large piece of cardboard. He hung it precariously from a knot in the ceiling, next to hoop skirts, a nun's robe, and harlequin pants.

Janco sat at the table, crafting a mask that looked like a monster, and Tzara, who had arrived late, made a mess of tiny words he clipped from a newspaper column. Arp, in an act that looked almost like anger, tore up a drawing he was working on and threw the pieces on the floor.

Emmy was still partial to the idea of it all and was almost starting to develop a slight aversion to the performance. Hugo was always so busy, directing his own world. And for a moment, she doubted he would miss her presence if she were no longer part of it.

Around five o'clock, Emmy started to get restless when everyone was still at their apartment, and she was supposed to go meet Vayo. Then, in a subtle act of defiance, she decided to sneak out. She told herself that no one would miss her anyway.

When she stepped outside, she breathed in the air. It was brisk and had a spicy smell of risk and freedom. She looked up at the Swiss sky, looking for the moon, but the sky was dark, and she realized the moon was new.

The streetlamps were glowing with a subtle orange light, which lit up the cobblestones that lead to the Zurich lake. She thought about what she would say when she saw Vayo again.

The night was dark without the moon, and the lake was eerie despite the swans, which swam by gracefully. Emmy found a bench under a lamp where she could sit and wait for the journalist. But then she saw something in the trees that distracted her.

It was her grandmother. Sitting on a branch of the tallest tree! Legs dangling, without any teeth.

"Grandmother?" Emmy exclaimed in surprise at the night sky. She stared at the tree, too scared to stand.

The old woman looked down at her without saying a word. Emmy shivered and wondered if she was dreaming.

Then, with the breeze, the vision disappeared, and Emmy pulled her coat around her to protect her from the chill.

She blinked a few times and then looked around. The journalist still wasn't there. Nobody was, which Emmy found peculiar, considering how early in the evening it was.

Maybe her grandmother was trying to warn her of something, Emmy thought. Then her heart started racing, and she started to get nervous. Maybe she should have never left. From her apartment, her home, from Germany.

She couldn't stand it a minute longer. Emmy got up from the bench and ran home. Her short hair blew in the frigid air, her green sweater scratched her skin. She thought she could cry, but she was too much in shock. And when she finally reached home, nobody was there.

***

She thought about what she should do, then went back toward where she had come from. When she reached Bellevue, the junction just before the lake, she saw Hugo through the windows of the Café Odeon at a small table in the corner. He was standing and talking to another man and Tzara was sitting in a chair across from him.

Emmy pushed open the door and felt the heat rise in her face.

"Hugo," she interrupted, almost crying. "The dreams I had about my grandmother. It was true. It was a warning." She was shaking.

Hugo looked at her as if he were trying to comprehend.

"Tonight, in the park," she said. "I went for a walk, and I saw her watching me from the trees. I saw her. It was a warning."

"Emmy?" he said. "Are you okay?"

"My grandma never comes to me, Hugo," Emmy said frantically. "As a child, I used to go to her grave and wait for her angel, but no angel ever came. My schoolmates used to tell me that angels appear only when necessary, just to console me."

"Maybe you should go to a fortune teller and ask her what it means," Tzara said, laughing.

"That would not work," Emmy said, glaring at him. She almost started to cry, then she turned to Hugo.

"Hugo, what should I do?"

"Emmy, are you sure you didn't smoke anything?" Tzara asked, still laughing.

The others were silent and looked at Hugo, who clearly showed his annoyance with Tzara. He looked at him angrily, then locked eyes with Emmy, proving in that moment just how much he loved her.

"Well," he replied, "Yes, it sounds like your grandmother is worried about you. Maybe she simply came to see how you were doing."

He reached out for her hand and held it tight in his. "Come," he said. "Let's go home."

38

Annemarie

Hugo tried to calm Emmy down. Everything was fine, he told her, and she was probably just exhausted. The daily performances were crippling, also for him. He, too, sometimes trembled in front of the crowds and thought about running away.

He told her that they could take a break. The cabaret could use a rest. But then, the next morning, she received a letter from her cousin, which said her mother was dead.

Emmy threw herself on the bed and cried over a pile of clothes. Silk, chiffon, cardboard, and cotton caught her tears as they overflowed. She cried not only out of grief but also because she feared, once again, that she wasn't strong enough to endure all that life demanded of her. Even though, deep down, she had always known her weaknesses and strengths since childhood.

***

From an early age, Emmy had lived in fear and shame, not knowing if life was a sin or a blessing. It is unfortunate for an unmarried girl to have a child, she was told after her son was born. As it was to gamble and be an actress, according to her mother. And yet, Emmy had chosen a life of freedom.

Unlike her son, who was born a sick baby after a difficult birth, her daughter Annemarie was born without any problems. Shortly after her birth, while Emmy was traveling with a troupe of actors, little Annemarie was blessed by a group of traveling gypsies. As they passed through town, they sang her soft, dreamy lullabies.

Like most times in her life, Emmy didn't have much money when Annemarie was born, and she had to sell the wedding ring from her ex-husband to buy a stroller. Emmy remembered how cute her little baby was when she was playing with a rattle — more than 10 years ago now. And how much she had looked like her father, a singer from Hungary, from the moment she was born.

Emmy believed at the time that Annemarie's father was the one person she would love forever, but like most things in life, he, too, was temporary. After a short time together, they went their separate ways. The last time she saw him, he had disappeared over the horizon, carrying his pet guinea pig in his arms.

Emmy's mother, God bless her soul, was a short-sighted, old-fashioned woman who was traditional and critical. Emmy hadn't initially told her mother about her granddaughter being born. She just arrived home one day carrying her baby in a cardboard box.

She remembered how angry her mother had been at the time and how Emmy had tried to calm her down. They met on the train platform, and Emmy was wearing a poppy-colored chiffon hat. The baby smiled at her grandmother from the box, which was covered by a veil that dancers wore on stage. Emmy begged her mother not to be angry for at least the first hour and told her how she missed her.

Emmy remembered how her mother had been hesitant to take them in at first, so Emmy had told her that Annemarie's father was her ex-husband — who had also fathered her late son. It wasn't true, but Emmy didn't think it mattered. It was her mother who felt shame among people who gossiped. Emmy didn't.

Throughout their visit, Emmy's mother tried to get her to stay home and get a decent job, but Emmy was eager to return to Munich and see the world. All she could think about was wanting to sing, write and dance. She had planned to take Annemarie with her, but her mother insisted on keeping the baby. So, Emmy left without her.

***

"It's okay," Hugo said, trying to make room on the bed to sit down. The room was a mess from the group's art and costume party. "We'll get through it." He held his hand on her back.

But it wouldn't be, she thought. This was just the beginning, and now everything would change.

"I'll get a permit to travel to Germany and get Annemarie," he said. "Or I can ask my sister to bring her here to Zurich."

Emmy was unable to speak. She could barely breathe well enough to keep her heart beating. Not only did she wonder how to get Annemarie to Switzerland, but also if her daughter even wanted to be with her. She hadn't seen her in years, and it had been months since she had written to her. She dwelled on the maternal responsibilities she had for so long neglected.

And my poor mother, she thought. Emmy didn't even have a passport to attend her funeral in Germany.

There was no one left in her hometown of Flensburg who could help her, only the distant cousin who had written and a half-sister who hated to travel. She wondered who else could help — Rudi, Erich, Hardy, or Else. Emmy panicked the longer she couldn't think of a solution.

"It's okay," Hugo said, rubbing her back softly. "Everything will be okay. I'll make sure of it."

253

39

-isms

As Emmy and Hugo carried the wardrobe for that night's show through Neiderdorf's dark alleys, her cries echoed loudly through the narrow alleys.

It had snowed that day. Big, round snowflakes, but before sunset, the snow had started to melt. Now, there was only mud and cold puddles on the broken cobblestones.

It was a few hours before the show, and Emmy was still crying. On the way to the cabaret, passers-by slowed their pace and watched as if they were already putting on a performance.

Colorful fabrics floated in the air. Hugo led the way like a general marching in the dark. He carried the clothes rack, which was twice his size. His cardboard suit was covered by a thin paper bag.

Emmy wasn't sure if she could go on, but she wanted to try for him.

"That's it," Hugo suddenly said and stopped. "Listen..."

Emmy looked at him, tears streaming down her face. She tried to stifle her sobs and be quiet.

"No," he said. "Cry."

"What?" Emmy looked at him with teary eyes.

"Never mind," he said, putting the coat rack down on the ground. He went to Emmy and kissed her forehead.

"I was just thinking about the laws of rhythm," he said. "For example, when the melody stops but its energy is still there, and then everyone starts talking at the same time."

Emmy didn't understand. It had started to rain, the streets were crowded, and it was cold. The only thing she could feel was a sharp pain in her heart.

Hugo squeezed her hands. "Thank you," he said. Then, he returned to the front to lead them forward.

***

When they reached the cabaret, the others were already there. The five of them who always talked over one another: Arp, Huelsenbeck, Tzara, Janco, and

Hugo — and to be honest, most of the time, her. They never agreed on the next big idea. They were constantly arguing and pushing each other's borders.

"Hugo!" Tzara sprang out of his chair and charged toward him. It was him versus Arp now, and he was seeking alliances. "We've been waiting for you, what took you so long? I wanted to talk to you about my idea for a publication."

"Well, I also have an idea," Huelsenbeck said loudly across the room. "... or maybe it was actually an idea of yours..."

Hugo shook his head, his arms full of costumes and props. "I don't know," he said. "I also have some things I need to figure out. Why don't we all just draw up an alphabetical list of our most frequent theories and ideas so we can continue production without constant interruptions?"

And then he dropped all the stuff in his arms. Hats, buckets, coats, and shoes fell onto the floor with a bang. He kicked at the pile, sending his shoe flying across the room. Then he picked up a top hat and put it on.

Everyone got quiet, waiting anxiously to see what Hugo would do. But he just sat on a windowsill, crossing his legs in the air, baring his bony ankles.

"Actually..." Tzara said after allowing Hugo a moment. He spoke softly. "That's what I'm proposing. We should write down everything. Start a journal."

"Why?" Hugo asked. "What we are doing here is not important to be printed."

Emmy looked at Hugo and wondered if that was true. She remembered how often he had complained about not being able to publish his work.

"This is about life!" he said rather angrily. "Life is more important. Life in and with the people. Socialism."

"We at least need a name," Huelsenbeck said, speaking from the far table in the corner. "No one knows what to call us. The newspapers still call us 'nihilists.'"

"Nihilism is not a cause, but just the logic of decadence," Hugo said. "Nietzsche said that."

No one responded. Hugo went on.

"Our cabaret is a gesture," he said. "Don't you understand? Every word that is spoken and sung here says only one thing: that this humiliating age has not succeeded in winning our respect."

The troupe listened, bowed heads, and nodded.

"Why do we need a name anyway?" Hugo asked. "What should they call us? 'Voltaire Society'? We are not special. What is special about us? Our big drums? Or is it our *idealism*, which has previously only been considered a joke?! Or maybe it is our spontaneous foolishness to put on this show? Is that it? Surely, our enthusiasm for illusion will destroy them as they continue their grandiose slaughters and cabalistic exploits."

"What we should do..." Hugo said in a final breath, "is discard the Ego like a beloved suit that you don't truly need anymore."

The others stayed quiet, and then Tzara spoke up.

"Da..." Tzara nodded and repeated loudly. "Da!" Janco was whispering into Tzara's ear, who was looking at Hugo.

"I understand what you're saying," Tzara said, now talking to Hugo. "But... 'Da, da!' He looked at Janco. "Yes! I know"

"Da, da?" Emmy asked. "What are you saying? You sound like a baby."

Tzara turned his attention to her. "'Da,'" he said. "Means 'yes' in Romanian — if you must know."

"That's funny," Huelsenbeck replied. "Because the French call 'Dada' a hobby horse. The ones that little kids ride on, made from a stick with a stuffed head."

"Yes, yes," Hugo said, annoyed by the direction of the conversation. "DADA is also the best Lilly milk soap in the world!"

Emmy remembered the shampoo ad they saw the night they had tried to sell his suit. The beautiful woman's long, thick, flowing hair that Emmy was dying to have.

"Don't you get it?" Hugo said. "This is not about foolish naivety or joy in procreation. A name would mean we stood for something, and how can that be when words mean nothing? Words has become a commodity. They have lost all dignity."

"What about Dada-ism?" Huelsenbeck suddenly suggested with wide, shining eyes.

"No, no, -isms!" Hugo was yelling now. "What we call DADA is a farce of nothingness in which all higher questions are involved; a gladiator's gesture, a play with shabby leftovers, the death warrant of posturing morality and abundance."

Then, he continued as if he was delivering a sermon.

"We must keep a good distance between ourselves and the world," he said, "because taking too close of interest in politics, public opinion, or what people are talking about is a fast route to aggravation, danger, and mental unwellness."

He went on about how life is a mix of the extraordinary and absurd. The contradictions, the destruction, the unnaturalness, and the primitive.

Everyone sat listening as if they were in a midnight mass.

"Humans are just troublesome and will never achieve the degree of logic, goodness, and kindness we long for," Hugo continued. Then, he went over to Emmy and put his arm around her shoulder.

"We should never tie our personal moods to the condition of a whole nation or people in general; otherwise, we will be set to weep continuously," he said. "We need to live in our own minds and keep ourselves busy with projects that keep us weary but satisfied. We should give up on cultivating the whole of humanity rather than take a few acres and make those your focus. A small orchard that grows lemons and apricots. Stop worrying about humanity and start caring for ourselves."

"Amen!" Huelsenbeck yelled. Then, they all got up to rehearse.

Intermission

Nothing,
but, also,
Everything,

        happens in this scene.

Just imagine dancing,

                  singing,

Yelling!
noisemaking, mask-wearing.

     The Balalaika band,
Big drums beating.
Consider it a gesture,

       from the cabaret,

                 to you.

40

The Star of the Cabaret

"Viva DADA!" A door slammed. Another one opened. "Viva DADA!"

Emmy walked slowly behind Arp and Tzara, who were pulling open doors and yelling "Viva DADA!" into small shops and restaurants.

They called it "mild publicity," but Emmy found it slightly embarrassing, even though she always claimed she didn't care what others thought of her.

Emmy hid behind a pillar, waiting for the other two to move on. That evening, they were scheduled to have their first big performance at the prestigious theater, *Zunfthaus zur Waage*. There would be poems, a Chant négres, and three "dada" dances by her, which she would perform wearing one of Janco's masks and accompanied by Hugo on piano.

Now, Arp and Tzara said, they were trying to get the word out.

**

Emmy was still awaiting news about when Annemarie would arrive, but it had been arranged that Emmy's half-sister would bring her to the border. Hugo had taken care of the logistical arrangements without worrying Emmy about the details.

She had been trying to imagine what life would be like when her daughter got to Zurich while also trying to accept all the unpredictability. She had tried to rid herself of her ego, as Hugo had suggested, but right now, her main focus was simply calming her nerves. It had helped that it was spring now, and Zurich was in bloom. And she was surrounded by young men who wanted to cause a scene, which made life, more or less, a little more fun.

As she, Arp, and Tzara continued walking alongside the river, the shop windows started to glow. The low sun on the horizon reflected on the panes. The steeple of the Fraumünster church that rose high into the sky was silhouetted against heaven's majestic pink and purple backdrop. And just before the sun set, it offered bright spots along the gray sidewalk with direct rays of light.

Emmy stepped out of the shadows. The beams kissed her face and warmed her soul. She was empowered, now, to shine.

***

When they finally arrived at the theater, the *Zunfthaus zur Waage*, it was as if everyone important in Zurich was already there. They made their way through the wide entrance hall as friends and strangers stopped to greet them.

Emmy smiled politely at acquaintances and strangers and stopped to chat with those who caught her attention. She wore a black silk dress with a plunging neckline. It was modern and elegant and gave her an aura of mystery.

She wasn't quite sure how the evening would play out, which is what she told everyone who asked what to expect from the show. What she didn't say was that the printed program was only *pro forma* because they themselves never knew exactly what was going to happen. All she knew was that this time, she would be helping Hugo stage a new genre of verse.

Arp's girlfriend, Sophie, had helped with the choreography, which at first Emmy found obscure and awkward, but then she began to appreciate the freedom her dances allowed for, especially when Emmy could hide behind one of Janco's terrifying masks.

For Emmy, performing was always about seducing the audience, both with her voice and her female form. She appreciated the avant-garde interpretations of a woman's body – even when dressed in cardboard and dancing like a machine.

***

"Da, da, Da-da!"

That was her sign. Emmy and Sophie came onto the stage, their bare feet tapping the floor lightly like nervous little ducks. Her arms and fingers were in long cardboard tubes. Emmy moved her arms from side to side in slow, angular movements.

At first, they moved with Hugo's rhythm but in opposite directions. Then, together, they tilted their bodies like falling chimneys before moving into angular, fragmented motions, contradicting his direction.

Emmy could well imagine the audience had never seen anything like it. Her face was hidden behind a horrible mask with an open mouth and a nose pressed to the side. There were important Swiss people in the audience: Franz Jelmoli and his daughter, Fritz Brupbacher, and Sophie's dance teacher, Rudolf Laban. Emmy wondered if they would realize the anti-bourgeoisie themes were really about them.

What she wanted to tell the audience, if she were the director, was that life was about living in the moment, free of shame or embarrassment. Free of expectations and validations, and freedom of one's self. Free from judgment, free to love — in all languages and with all talents.

After all, there could be nothing more shameful than what was happening in the rest of the world.

Except maybe — it suddenly occurred to her — that she was a bad mother.

Emmy had been told that her singing could captivate anyone who would hear her, but now she wasn't singing. Instead, she just…

"Agghhhhh!!!"

…let out a terrible scream.

41

Karawane

"Language has been misused!" Hugo yelled out to the crowd. He was standing in the middle of the stage on top of an oriental rug.

It wasn't magic, but there was something magical up his sleeve, which was made of cardboard and wrapped around him like a column. His legs were also pillars, painted blue, and he wore a tall cylindrical cap that was open at the top. A gold paper collar, which he also made himself, was draped around his shoulders like a superhero's cape.

Emmy stood backstage, watching Hugo perform. She had changed back into her black dress, which allowed her to breathe. Her scream had been directed.

It wasn't only in her head. And now… it was Hugo's turn to act.

In front of him were three music stands facing the audience. On top of each was his manuscript, which he had written in red pencil. As he began officiating, at one podium, then another, the audience sat quietly, observing in wonder.

"You have to take the words apart; get to the bottom of them!" Hugo said, his pale face half-frightened, half-curious. Emmy wondered if he should have worn one of Janco's masks as well.

"If you do…" Hugo continued, "You find surprising associations go against the usual clichés. Against a mentality that makes war possible."

Emmy knew Hugo's renouncement of language was a nod against journalists like Vayo, just as much as it was about the general conversation around death and destruction. He asked everyone to give up words that they didn't invent themselves to reject ideas, jokes, and images invented by others. Admit that language had been abused and corrupted.

In case the audience had forgotten, they were reminded of the war that was raging nearby. The Battle of Verdun was in its fourth month, and there had recently been a German assault on the French along the Western front. Flamethrowers, stormtroopers, poisonous gas, and hand grenades were now words being reported in the papers.

Suddenly, Hugo started flapping his arms like a bird with stiff cardboard wings. While this caused a commotion, Emmy looked at the audience, who—at least—looked more shocked than bored. Then, slowly and majestically, Hugo began his speech, increasing the emphasis on the sounds of the consonants.

"Elefanten Karawane." He read the title first.

"jolifanto bambala ô falli…"

By the middle of the verse, he was overcome with emotion. Sweat dripped down his forehead as if he had been caught in heavy rains, but he kept a straight face, maintaining his composure.

Then, he began to chant his vows in a kind of religious way. The audience listened intently at Hugo's words, which flowed freed from traditional syntax. His words, baseless vowels with irrational breaks. Repetitive, splintered constructions in foreign pronunciations. It was the first abstract phonetic poem. A poem of sounds, not words.

"ba – umf," Hugo said. Then, the room went black and Emmy, Janco, Arp, and Tzara rushed onto the stage to carry Hugo away.

High in the sky, dripping with sweat, Hugo smiled down at Emmy in peace. Floating, like a magical bishop, worshiped with the sound of a roaring applause.

42

Flaws, or Fate

Emmy, Hugo, and Annemarie were alone in the Cabaret Voltaire, but while it was empty there was a familiar feeling of heartwarming safety. Emmy wondered if Voltaire would be proud of what they were doing. Whether the name they had given themselves would endure or fade away.

Life moved so quickly, she realized, thinking back to where she had been since Annemarie's birth—not just where she had come from, but also where she had performed. *That*, she thought, Voltaire would be proud of. It was he who said, "Life is a shipwreck, but we must not forget to sing in the lifeboats."

She looked at Hugo, knowing his amusements had never done harm to the world. Even Annemarie seemed to sense how great his beautiful soul was. The child had practically flown to him the first moment they met. Maybe, she realized, there were things one was destined to do that they were powerless against, such as being a daughter or mother.

***

Emmy looked at Annemarie, who was sitting with Hugo at one of the long wooden tables in the middle of the room. They were painting with large brushes in strong primary colors. Hugo showed Annemarie his canvas, which made the child giggle. She had dark hair like her father's, but her bangs were cut across her forehead in the same way as Hugo's.

Hugo smiled at the girl, then looked up at Emmy.

It was a beautiful friendship between her daughter and Hugo. All of the Dadaists, really, had been overly kind since Annemarie's arrival, Emmy realized. They seemed to appreciate the childlikeness as an art as much as Annemarie was fascinated by the atmosphere.

"Good evening, Miss Artist-in-residence," Arp said as he arrived at the cabaret. He had come in through the back-alley door, as they all did now.

He walked over to the table where Hugo and Annemarie were sitting, examining their art. Annemarie had painted a kaleidoscope of blue butterflies in the sky. "A masterpiece! We shall hang this on the wall."

"Really?" Annemarie asked. "Is it really good enough?"

"Good enough?!" he said. "You're already the best!"

The child laughed and blushed.

"Here," he said. "I've saved you something sweet." He took out a crumbled piece of strawberry cake from his jacket pocket and gave it to her.

"You know," he said. "Abstract art will destroy formalism."

The girl looked at him, wide-eyed and bemused.

"Watch…" Arp took a piece of paper from the table and cut it into a circle, then folded it in half and cut a half-circle in the middle. Then, he opened it up, held it to his eye, and peeked through the little hole as if it were a monocle. "We should not concern ourselves so much with richness as with simplification," he said.

Annemarie laughed, but Emmy wondered if he was making fun of Tzara, who often wore a monocle as a fondness for dandyism.

"Maybe," Hugo said. "Unless the abstract age is over."

"What do you mean?" Arp looked offended.

"Don't worry," Hugo said. "It's not a bad thing. In fact, it is a great triumph of art over the machine."

"Are you suggesting our attempts to remove ourselves from the inculcated, traditional forms of art have been in vain?"

"No," Hugo said. "Just that one can only fully understand a Rembrandt during a Catholic service, in the candlelight of an illuminated dome."

"But our show was a hit."

"It doesn't matter!" Hugo said, slamming his hands down on the table. The child flinched, but he didn't notice. "That's the point. The present does not exist in principles, only in association. Just this morning, I heard from Germany that inflation has made the bourgeoisie the lowest class. There is no longer a middle class like before the war. The *gentlemen* have become weak. Dandyism is now a school of paradox."

"Is that true?" Emmy asked. She placed her hand on Annemarie's back to signal everything was okay.

"It's how it is now," he said, confirming his words. "In the streets, at the cafés and the storefronts in Germany. There are no more fat masters at the Café des Westens. Only some soldiers, a few girls, and plants. 'C'est tout.'"

"C'est tout," Annemarie repeated in French.

Hugo looked at her, then smiled sadly. "It means, 'That's it. It's finished.'"

43

Manifesto

Hugo's manifesto, which he read aloud at Cabaret Voltaire just four months after its opening day, was more than a thinly disguised break.

***

In fact, he later proudly declared in his diary it was "the first manifesto of a newly founded cause known to refute the cause itself to its supporter's face."

He called DADA "terribly simple" and "quite easy to understand." It was a "World War without end," a "revolution without beginning."

"Dada Tzara, dada Huelsenbeck, dada m ' dada, dada m ' dada dada mhm, dada dera dada, dada Hue, dada Tza," he said. "How does one achieve eternal bliss? By saying DADA. How does one become famous? By saying DADA."

He even went as far as to tell the audience exactly how he created the magic. How he formed his words:

"I just let the vowels simply occur, like a cat meowing," he said. "Words emerge, shoulders of words, legs, arms, hands of words. Au, oi, uh."

The reaction was silence.

"It's the word," he said, almost defeated. "The word, gentlemen, that is a public concern of the first importance."

44

A Piece of Human History

Even before Hugo had finished his manifesto, everyone realized that he was leaving. His words, once a mystery to so many, were now laid out clearly.

After his performance, Emmy had tried to convince him of his success. To assure him that he had fulfilled his wish to restore art to its original, magical power. But Hugo just said that it was done. The Cabaret Voltaire was no longer the right stage for him.

"Are you sure?" Emmy asked before giving up.

"When things are finished, I cannot spend any more time on them," he said. "That's just how I am."

"You can't go!" Huelsenbeck said with tears in his almond eyes.

They were all sitting at the cabaret at the long wooden table in the middle. Tzara, Janco, Hugo, Arp, Huelsenbeck and Emmy.

"Where are you going?" Tzara asked.

"Ticino," Hugo said.

"You can't leave," Huelsenbeck said. "Dada is your child."

"I didn't birth Dada," Hugo replied. "No one did. All Dada is, is a lamentable outburst. A disgraceful release of emotions and occurrence."

They all made a heavy sigh and prepared for another one of his sermons.

"Our attempt of adopting symmetries and rhythms instead of principals is too abstract to make an impact," he said. He told them how he wanted to re-consider the importance of language that could be used to shape an intellectual's thoughts. Use facts and truth to avoid what could be misconstrued. Avoid subordinate clauses, go back to verses, essays, and dramas. Press straight onward.

"We did nothing but dissolve language that had otherwise become rigid, corrupted, and discredited due to its use as propaganda," he continued. "But European skepticism and phantasm have undermined even Catholicism in Germany. We must break through to tradition, and that means negating whole centuries of national development. Build on the intelligence of individual symbols, prevent the mills of banality from turning."

"But Hugo," Huelsenbeck said. "We *are* the German Intelligence."

Tzara rose from the bench and pushed it away from the table. "And what are we supposed to do with you gone? Dismantle? Dada belongs to everybody. Like the idea of God or the toothbrush."

"I don't care what you do," Hugo said. "Start your publication."

"I will," Tzara replied. "And I will print it in Zurich."

"Good," Hugo said. "Call it 'Dada.'"

They stared at each other, and the others were silent.

"Dada, Dada, Dada," Hugo said, standing up to march around the room. "How does one achieve eternal bliss? By saying, Dada." Then, he started reciting his Manifesto again. "Dada is a new tendency in art. It is *terribly* simple…"

"What about Emmy?" Huelsenbeck asked, over Hugo's speech. "If not for her songs, we will starve to death."

Emmy looked at Huelsenbeck sadly, warmed by what he said, but she didn't say anything. Her silence gave him her answer.

"I think I'm going to be sick," he said.

45

Parting

"My dear Emmyline," Hugo wrote. "Thank you so much for being there and for helping me escape."

Hugo had arrived in Ticino exhausted, he explained in his letter, but like Robinson Crusoe, on a grand adventure. He said he was happy and impressed by the beauty of the place, where locals strolled around in sandals and tunics.

"Tell Tzara that Ticino is more beautiful than Zurich, Dada, and all related things," he wrote. "And I hereby declare all Expressionism, Dadaism, and other - isms the worst of the bourgeoisie. Evil, evil, evil."

He also called the cabaret "useless," "bad," "decadent," and "militaristic." Then, he signed the letter, "Your Hugo."

"P.S. Come as soon as you can."

***

Emmy sat in their apartment in Zurich reading the letter. The room was almost empty except for a few cardboard boxes and hangers.

Like Hugo, the Cabaret Voltaire was never the solution for Emmy, but she did find it a bit dramatic to end the Dada chapter so abruptly. She was sad to leave Zurich and say goodbye to everyone, even Tzara. They had all played a role together. One she didn't want to forget.

She put the letter down and looked over at her daughter, who was folding clothes neatly into the small suitcase that she had arrived to Zurich with.

Emmy had told Hugo to go ahead to Ticino and that she would stay and organize the move. When he found an apartment, she told him he should write to her, which he did.

Now it was time. Once again, she had to accept a new fate. A new chapter as a family would begin in a new place.

And while Emmy wasn't quite sure what was coming next, she was content in her hope of hope. Ready for the next adventure. Like a tightrope walker in the dark.

But before they left, she had one more stop to make.

***

As expected, as soon as Hugo departed, Tzara took the lead of the Dadaist's future. He immediately started working on the publication and even organized a new venue for their performances and exhibitions. They moved from Niederdorf to Paradeplatz, the most expensive part of the city.

Emmy held Annemarie's hand as they crossed the tram tracks, past Credit Suisse and the Baur en Ville, the most magnificent grand hotel in the city. Emmy wasn't sure if she got the address right, but Tzara had told her it was near the banks in the home of the Sprüngli café, which was famous for its chocolate.

It was still morning when they arrived at the Gallery Dada. Emmy knocked gently on the door as Annemarie pressed her face against the glass.

"Look, mama!" she said. "I see my painting."

She was jumping up and down excitedly as Tzara opened the door.

"Welcome to the Gallery, Dada," he said, guiding them into the hall. Sunlight bounced off the white walls and parquet floors.

They went over to Annemarie's painting first. A landscape inspired by French Impressionism.

There were futurist and cubist paintings as well, including works by Arp and Janco. There were sculptures from Africa on brightly colored stools and surreal geometric worlds by de Chirico.

The gallery was adventurous, Emmy thought. She liked how Tzara had designed it. It was brilliant, actually, opening the gallery at Paradeplatz, she thought. It was as if he were bending the rules of high society without transgressing them. Just like a dandy.

"I brought you something," Emmy said, reaching into her bag. She handed him two puppets that she had made. "They're named 'Zar' and 'Zaress,' and they know all the answers to all of the problems." She smiled as she gave them to him. "Dada, our joy and problem child right up to the end."

"We won't stop performing," Tzara replied. "Even without Hugo. We'll get louder. They'll hear us in Berlin, Paris, and even in New York."

"I wish it to be true," Emmy said. "And with each story of success, I will shout proudly from wherever I am, 'Long Live Dada!'"

46

The Last Reckoning

Swinging and jumping. Laban girls in ugly costumes, oversized, wearing Janco's scary masks. Brisés and pirouettes.

"Against, without, for Dada!" screams Hans Richter from Berlin.

"Malicious, elegant, Dada, Dada, Dada!" replies Tzara from Paris.

Twenty people singing a poem simultaneously off-key.

```
          Do              Mi
    Re                    Do
          Mi Do
    Re                    Re
    Mi      Do    Do
                          Do
```

The outraged audience boos and screams. An inverted urinal on display in New York City. They cheer and laugh and jump onto the stage. They tear down gilded banisters and balustrades.

A mannequin with a head full of flowers flies across the room in Zurich, sending pink and purple petals through the air.

Glass shatters on the floor.

Another: "Woop! Hooray!"

Noise, music. Nothing at all. Only the energy of the times. The moment.

Epilogue

Ticino, Switzerland
May 1934

The soft clicking of the keys stopped. Emmy pulled the sheet of paper out of the typewriter, put it on the thick stack beside it, and, after glancing at the framed photo on the wall, came back to the present. The picture showed a smiling Annemarie with an infant in her arms.

Emmy still wasn't sure if she wanted to respond to the *Neue Zürcher Zeitung's* request. Capturing her memories of the places she had lived, of who she had been. Everything that had led to the here and now was for herself.

***

When, after three years in Ticino, she had decided to marry Hugo, the fate of both of them became one. Anything they were afraid to lose, they were determined to risk together.

Around the same time, the war had ended. But then, Hugo died at the age of only 41.

After his death, Emmy was certain that she, too, would die soon, but the days just moved on. Some dark, some light.

Life, Emmy reflected, is always a fine line. Darkness on one side, light and love on the other.

She looked at the baby in the photo who looked out onto the world with hope and optimism. Annemarie had given birth in January and named her child "Hugo" out of loving memory.

Emmy wished she could tell the baby all of life's secrets, but she had never thirsted for life's knowledge to ease her worries. There were always reasons for optimism, she considered. Even Voltaire believed all human suffering was part of the cosmic plan. And Hugo, who always insisted on being introspective, hadn't been completely critical of life either.

If she had learned nothing else from life's uncertainties, it was that in the morning, the sun would rise, and the birds once more would sing. And that the love one gives another can illuminate the way through the darkness, like a small ray of light.

Afterword

The initial view that success in war would create strength for the winners proved true in a sense but in contradictory expectations and unexpected fashion.

When the fighting of World War 1 ended in November 1918, returning to the normal and familiar created an urgent need for a new kind of unity. A desire to return to the good old days of pre-1914 meant a more conservative view among citizens. Those who weren't fulfilled by the outcome of the fight now saw war as a promoter of change, including the Bolsheviks, led by Lenin, who left Zurich and began the Social Revolution in Russia.

By July 1919, many of the Dadaists were told to go back to their own countries. Switzerland was to be a "transit point" for the displaced and vulnerable rather than a "permanent haven," the government asserted.

Huelsenbeck went to Berlin, Tzara to Paris, and Arp to Cologne, bringing with them their ideas of Dada. Intent on spreading the -ism that was never meant to exist.

***

Huelsenbeck took the reins of the Dada government in Berlin, joining a post-war Germany in their progressive thinking. He delivered Dada speeches about the "artistic movement" founded in Zurich with manifestos and galleries and provocative political statements. Eventually, this led to its denouement as *Kunstbolschewismus*, or Cultural Bolshevism, by German National Socialists, which led to Huelsenbeck being repeatedly investigated by Nazi authorities. Secularist, modern, and progressive cultures were denounced, and Huelsenbeck was forbidden to write or make art. He remained in 'internal exile' until receiving a visa in 1936 and immigrating to the United States to practice medicine. In 1970, he returned to Switzerland, where he lived for four years in Ticino until he passed away.

Tzara became the "President of Dada" in France, aligning himself with idealism and creating a legacy that would long impact the future of Cubism, Futurism, the Beat Generation, Situationism, and Rock. Politically active for the majority of his life, Tzara also supported a communist vision and joined the French Resistance during World War II. He spoke in favor of liberation and aligned himself with the cause of anti-fascism until he was forced to seek exile in the south of France. He survived with a group of artists and philosophers, protected by an American diplomat. He stayed active and was honored for his work until he passed away quietly in his Parisian home at age 67.

Arp and Sophie married and continued to make art, establishing the Cologne Dada group, before also moving to Paris. Arp joined a group of Abstraction-Créationists to counteract the influence of Surrealists and moved from collage to sculpture while writing essays and poems. In 1942, the couple returned to Zurich to escape German occupation in France, where Sophie died a year later in her sleep from accidental carbon monoxide poisoning. Her legacy remains one of the most important influencers of concrete art and geometric aspirations. She was honored for years by her home country of Switzerland, who featured her portrait on the 50 Swiss franc banknote.

Erich Mühsam stayed in Germany and remained true to his reputation of being a rebel. In 1933, he was arrested on unknown charges and labeled a "Jewish subversive" and communist agitator by Joseph Goebbels, the Nazi Minister of Propaganda. He died in a Nazi prison after being beaten for weeks. It was reported that his teeth were broken by musket blows, a swastika was branded on his scalp, and he was forced to dig his own grave. The reports also claim he sang until his last days.

Else fled Nazi Germany and lived the remainder of her life in Jerusalem. **Lottie** became famous for her dolls and worked as a costume designer for Wedekind until she withdrew from public life in the 1930s after being exposed as the daughter of a presumed Jewish parent. **Rudi**, who remained famous for his drawings of Emmy, stayed in Berlin until he fled to Zurich in 1930, where he remained until his death.

The Nazis appointed **Laban** as their head of dance for the 1936 Olympics in their desire to show physical perfection. He never had the chance to direct the final show, however, after he too raised suspicions by Goebbels. In the midst of the investigation, Laban fled to England to seek refuge.

Hans Richter continued making art and later directed films in the Dada style, which the Nazis also destroyed and declared "degenerative art." He moved from Switzerland to the United States in 1940 and became an American citizen, then traveled back to Switzerland, where he too died in Ticino at age 87.

Janco is remembered as one of the leading Romanian Jewish intellectuals of his generation. He used his revolutionary vision to design some of the most innovative landmarks in downtown Bucharest. He married, had a daughter, and traveled happily around Europe until he, too, was targeted by antisemitic persecution. His work was called a prime example of "Jewish" and "bastard" art. During WW2, he sought refuge in British-occupied Palestine, where he continued to be involved in art movements. He died in Israel at age 88, highly regarded and awarded.

Hugo and Emmy remained in Ticino, where they married and lived in happy solitude until 1927 when Hugo died of stomach cancer at age 41. His final *Critique of the German Intelligentsia* was called a "piece of human history."

Emmy stayed eternally married to Hugo and dedicated years of her life to writing down their stories. And though she felt she might die without him, she outlived him for two decades.

A Definition

Dada /ˈdɑːdɑː/:

noun

noun: **Dada**

An early 20th-century movement in art, literature, music, and film, repudiating and mocking artistic and social conventions and emphasizing the illogical and absurd.

***

If one seeks a dictionary now to explain the word "Dada," one will discover it has a clear definition.

Yet, no one can describe exactly that feeling of rebellion, hidden behind suspicion and the desire to do what the troupe was passionate about at the time.

Despite Hugo's intentions, "Dada" evolved loudly into other -isms and, in the end, inspired multiple global movements across art and politics.

It impacted Italian Futurism, German Expressionism, and Surrealism and made a lasting impression on performance art. And, with works like *The Fountain*, Dada led to the discovery that it was possible to laugh again.

Beat Generation members Allen Ginsberg and William S. Burroughs credited their fragmented poetry as Dada-inspired. Artist Andy Warhol and *The Beatles'* John Lennon and Paul McCartney all said Dada made an impact on their work. David Bowie reportedly adopted Tzara's mannerisms and style during some of his performances, as well as Radiohead and Damien Hirst. David Byrne of *The Talking Heads* said the song "I Zimbra" and his 2020 Broadway show, *American Utopia*, both have hints of Dadaism at its core.

And so, it continues as Dada made its mark on punk-rock, post-punk, and trip-hop, the art of collage, Banksy, The Monty Python, modern comedy, and the acceptance of photography as art.

Yet still, if one asks, "What is Dada?" the answer shall remain and always be, "Nothing."

Author's Note

What was Beautiful and Good is a novel, a work of
fiction, inspired by the German poet and performer
Emmy Hennings and, in particular, her involvement
with the Cabaret Voltaire and Dada art movement.

I came to Emmy's story while living in Zurich,
Switzerland near the Cabaret Voltaire, which still exists
as a bar, museum and gathering space for performers
and artists. The historic buildings and cobblestone
pathways led me in the footsteps of Emmy, a woman
who inspired a generation of artists, optimists and
those striving for freedom.

In my research, I gained access to original artworks,
books, memoirs, poems and manifestos. Many of these
literary treasures were discovered at the museums and
libraries in Zurich, including the Cabaret Voltaire, the
Zentralbibliothek Zürich, the Kunsthaus library, and
Dr. Peter Bichsel Fine Books GmbH. Christa
Baumberger and Nicola Behrmann's biography, *Emmy
Hennings Dada*, published in collaboration with the
Schweizerische Literaturarchiv was also a great support
during my research.

This book is a passionate tribute to the remarkable
life of Emmy Hennings – a journey through her
poems, letters and novels that have captivated my heart
and soul. In writing this novel, I strove to be true to
Emmy's voice and innermost thoughts and have

included translated quotes from her and the other characters to honour their being.

Most, if not all, of my research was done in German, the original language of the documents. Original translations as well as objective anecdotes appear in this story.

On occasion, the actual words of Emmy Hennings, Hugo Ball, Tristan Tzara, Marcel Janco, Hans Arp, and other characters in this novel are used within dialogue exchanges or thoughts. Short phrases from original sources are also embedded throughout the narrative. These quotes have all been translated from the original language: German.

My use of documents and sources from these historical records are not intended to change the fictional nature of this work. While many events in this novel did occur, my interpretation is not meant to be definitely accurate.

Emmy, a muse to many, had a voice that exuded beauty and strength. Despite the limited opportunities for women in the early 20th Century, she fearlessly followed her heart and lived a life that was truly her own.

I sincerely hope that her extraordinary spirit and unique perspective comes across in the words of this novel.

Acknowledgements

I am immensely grateful to my steadfast support system—my friends and family—who stood by me through the often isolating and intense writing process. A heartfelt thank you to my dear friend and translator Christine K. Gubler, whose passion for the novel helped make it possible, and Judith Furrer for her tireless efforts. I would like to thank my publishers, Münster Verlag and Amazon Publishing for their belief in this work and their commitment to sharing it with the world.

To the city of Zurich, whose cobblestone streets and picturesque setting has remained the same for hundreds of years. I found inspiration in every corner of this city and was able to write this novel with help from the endless coffees at some of the same cafés that Emmy and her friends gathered.

To my dad, my mom, twin sister and brother, who are always there unconditionally. To my husband and son who have patiently waited for me to finish this dream before embarking on ours.

To the remarkable women who played a starring role in my life—Aneeqah, Ashley, Bekah, Becca, Brittany, Candace, Camilla, Cristina, Desirée, Kimberly, Kirsten, Melanie, Nancy, Pricilla, Rhonda, Vienna and countless others. You all beautifully embody the complexity and grace of femininity and have each left an indelible mark on my journey.

To the men who helped shape my story—Eric, who gave me the strength to follow this dream. Keith Roysdon, my editor and friend, Nathan, the brilliant writer, screenwriter Spenser, and Brian, the Pulitzer Prize-winning journalist who showed me the power of balance and passion. And to Andrew, Alex, Ben, Braden, Courtney, Kyle, Mike, Mike, Ryan and the extraordinary others who have touched my life over the years. You've all contributed to my view of the world. I am blessed to have had you in my life. I don't get the chance to tell you enough.

A special mention goes to David, who gifted me the 1999 print edition of *Publishing for Dummies* and the courage to pursue dreams that rearrange constellations. To Jade, my eternal best friend, and my niece, Avelyn, whose boundless spirit fills me with hope for the next generation of women. Together we can shape a world where dreams thrive, and voices are truly heard.

About the Author

Jill Blocker is a novelist and former journalist. She is the author of *What was Beautiful and Good* (*Was schön war und gut*).

She received a bachelor's degree in Journalism from Ball State University and studied creative writing through Stanford University's Continuing Studies program.

Originally from the U.S., she currently lives in Zurich, Switzerland with her husband and son.

Printed in the USA
CPSIA information can be obtained
at www.ICGtesting.com
LVHW080801080124
768326LV00030B/1702